The Quizzit family of London operated a shop called

### The Ark

Being a collection of wild and tame animals from all parts of the Globe, caught and rendered friendly by the Proprietor,

Joseph Quizzit.

The marvelous collection of animals included white mice, squirrels, a raccoon, a porcupine, jerboas, monkeys, a badger, an armadillo, a bear, an ape, hares and bats and fox cubs—and finally "that most unusual and almost extinct bird," the dodo, who was "not for sale but was regarded as the talisman or cornerstone of the whole business."

The Quizzit children, Verney and Theodosia, were accustomed to the din and chatter of the animals in the shop and so were all the more surprised when one evening the parrot said clearly to them: "If you two little Quizzits want to hear a good yarn to- to cower in some hole or nest as the winter weather gripped the countryside."

A strange turn of events brings about the happy future to be shared by the animals and the Quizzits.

RICHARD BOYDE is the pseudonym of a British artist and writer for adults. This is his first book for young readers.

*THE LAST DODO*

# The Last Dodo

## by Richard Boyde

*ILLUSTRATED BY THE AUTHOR*

Farrar, Straus & Giroux ✧ New York

*AN ARIEL BOOK*

# CONTENTS

# THE LAST DODO

# Chapter I

# MR. QUIZZIT'S SHOP

*O*NCE upon a time at the end of the reign of George III, there stood in London, hard by St. Paul's Churchyard, an animal shop. Over its front door, large yellow letters announced that it belonged to Mr. Joseph Quizzit. Above its portly bow window there swung a painted signboard. On one side was a picture of a spotted leopard prancing proudly across the sky. On the other the passerby could read, if he was able to, the following legend:

### THE ARK

Being a collection of wild and tame animals from all parts of the Globe, caught and rendered friendly by the Proprietor,

**JOSEPH QUIZZIT.**

OFFERED TO THE PUBLIC WITHOUT GUARANTEE,
but with the highest recommendations.

## BY APPOINTMENT TO HIS MAJESTIE'S COURT
Patronized by all the Best Families

The part about "without guarantee" was written very small, the next line very large, and the "BY APPOINTMENT" even larger. This was worded rather vaguely so that it could be taken, as Mr. Quizzit hoped it would be, to mean that His Royal Majesty was his patron. Actually he wasn't, but a monkey had once been purchased from his shop by Queen Anne's wigmaker, and he thought that quite a good enough excuse to qualify him for making such an announcement. So far no one had gainsaid him.

As soon as the shutters were taken down in the morning, a crowd of little boys were to be seen, gluing their noses to the windowpanes to find what animals were in stock. It was as good as a menagerie for them. If they were not straining their eyes to see the smallest mouse in the smallest cage in the farthermost corner of the shop, they were craning their necks and gazing up at the leopard on the signboard, their hands in their pockets and their hats on the backs of their heads. For in those days the sight of a shopful of animals was a very unusual thing; many of the children caught a glimpse for the first time in their lives of animals that they had never even seen pictures of. In fact, artists came regularly to Joseph Quizzit's shop to make pictures of his animals and birds. He was a stout North Countryman with a kindly eye who always had a civil word for the onlookers at the window.

Sometimes Mr. Quizzit would come out of the shop, in his leather apron and long-tailed stocking cap, with a monkey or a cat that he was in the act of dosing tucked under one arm.

Brandishing a large red-spotted duster at the crowd of boys and girls, he would drive them away, saying that they made such a crowd about his window that genuine buyers could not get near. Now and again one of the little boys would pluck up enough courage to go into the shop, clutching in his hot hand a threepenny bit or a groat, to ask the price of a Patagonian cavy or of a sweet singing bird, but usually he came out with only a white mouse or a box full of mulberry leaves and a few silk-worms. Prices were high and Mr. Quizzit, although very kind, could not often reduce them to suit the purses of his young customers. However, they had been in the shop and could tell their round-eyed friends of the wonders they had seen there, both real and imaginary.

One little girl came out saying she was sure she had seen the devil chained up by the neck in a far corner of the shop. He was wearing a short cape, she said, he had mouthed at her, and she swore that for her part she was not going into the shop again as long as she lived. She ran off down the street as fast as her legs would carry her, clutching a little box of butterflies she had bought for her sister's birthday. What she had really seen was a monkey with a most singular aspect, a dejected, homesick pro-boscis monkey, who had come all the way from Cochin China. He was covered with chestnut-colored hair that did actually grow longer around his shoulders like a cloak, and he had a strange long divided nose and a face marked with blue and red. He had, it is true, a human appearance, but the little girl must have taken a very hasty look. However, it served for a little while to keep some of the more timid boys away, and all the girls, so that passersby could at least tell from the window what sort of a shop it was.

In the summer Mr. Quizzit put a pile of wooden cages outside his shop, as bait to attract adult customers. Then the children had a free animal show without the hampering bottle glass of the window between them and the animals. They would gaze longingly at the cages of mice that had an upstairs and downstairs joined by a ladder; at the red squirrels who ran around and around a little treadmill with a frantic ecstasy of energy; at the hutches of parti-colored Dutch rabbits who munched solidly at their lettuce leaves; at the occasional spectacle of an aged wizened monkey who wore a red coat even on the hottest summer day; and at the cages of linnets bursting their poor sad hearts in a desperate effort to gain their freedom by sheer volume of song. Once there had been a talking parrot, but only once, for it caused such a crush and commotion that the sedan-chair men could not get by.

Mr. Quizzit employed a boy with sandy hair and freckles whose name was Silas. He had obtained this boy's services by applying for him through the charity authorities. Silas had been born in the debtor's prison of Newgate, and when judged old enough to leave his ailing mother, had been taken squalling from her and placed in a home for orphans. He had stayed there until Mr. Quizzit found him. He had grown from a sickly pink infant into a freckled spindly boy, meek by nature and put upon by all. He led an unhappy life in the orphanage, where he was bullied

6

by the other inmates and, because of his amenable disposition, imposed upon by the staff, who gave him all the hard and unpleasant tasks they shunned. It was therefore a great relief to him when Mr. Quizzit came one day to look the boys over and choose an assistant from among them. Because of his doleful expression and lack of surliness Mr. Quizzit had selected him and to the lad's surprise had even bought him a toffee apple from a stall on their way back to the shop. When they arrived there Mrs. Quizzit's eyes had characteristically filled with tears at the sight of the boy's gangling hungry look. She lost no time before settling him down at the Quizzits' family dinner table and stuffing him full of steak pudding and mashed potatoes, which practice she had been continuing for some time with no actual improvement to the boy's physique but a great improvement to his state of mind.

Mr. Quizzit soon realized that he had made an excellent choice, for Silas was as devoted an assistant as anyone could wish. It became his job, poor fellow, for he was little more than a child himself, to scare away the children by short sharp onslaughts at the cobbles in front of the shop with an old besom. When he was not at this task he fetched vegetable food from Covent Garden and pieces of offal from Smithfield with which to feed the stock. He carried bails of straw from the docks for the bottom of the animals' sleeping cages, sacks of sand and sawdust from the sawmill for the floor of the shop. He was not much good at his job of child scarer, for he liked to stop in his work to gaze at the animals as much as the other children did.

For in his case familiarity with the caged creatures certainly did not breed contempt but rather admiration at the patient way most of them put up with their imprisonment. He did not enjoy the office of jailer to all his family of prisoners, but he was kindhearted and gentle with them. He had been known to thrash a bullying boy soundly who poked a stick at a cage full of throstles.

The inside of the Quizzits' shop was packed from floor to ceiling with wooden, barred cages. Behind the shop was a small yard that contained a huge tank and a stable where much larger animals were kept. It had a loft above it in which Silas slept. At present the stable was occupied by two parti-colored tapirs who were not very pleasant bedfellows for Silas in the hot weather.

Joseph Quizzit was lucky in that he had no neighbors to complain of the noise his animals made, for on each side of his shop stood warehouses. The people who worked there made so much noise themselves during the day that they heard nothing. At night everyone went home, so that there were no complaints of the terrible racket that went on incessantly day and night.

Above the shop was the Quizzits' best parlor. Above this was another set of rooms in which Mr. and Mrs. Quizzit and the two children, their daughter Theodosia and their son Verney, all slept, or where sometimes they kept an overflow of stock. In a manner of speaking, they were surrounded and hemmed in by animals. Their smallest movement was followed by a hundred pairs of eyes. This did not discountenance them, for they were used to it and took no notice, but poor Silas was quite embarrassed and would, I believe, have let half the animals loose if he had owned the shop.

Mr. Quizzit, a man now past forty, had inherited the shop from his father, who was retired and lived at Mortlake and who had it in his turn from his father and he from his, for as far back as could be remembered. The present proprietor had before his marriage been engaged in catching the animals with which to stock the shop, and in so doing, had traveled both far and wide. Thus the horizons of his mind and understanding had been broadened, giving him a tolerance and perception extending further than the average man's, which qualities, with his wife's help, he was gently passing on to Theodosia and Verney, his children.

Arabella Quizzit, his wife, was as rosy-cheeked and plump as any good wife and mother should be. Brimming over with the warmth of easy tears and laughter, always cooking good, plain, copious meals and plumping out featherbeds and pillows, she had a natural aptitude for homemaking and made her husband very happy. He knew the contentment of unswerving love and devotion, so that he was able to apply himself to the care and collection of his stock without anxiety or complication. Arabella carried hot soup to the ailing and elderly of the parish, gossiped but little with the neighbors, tended the sick animals as tenderly as she did her own children, and taught both Silas and her son and daughter the catechism and what simple faith she herself believed in.

Theodosia, the elder of the two children, was dark-eyed,

black-haired, and quiet—reflective by nature. "Still waters run deep," her father used to say as he watched her sleeping, with her long lashes brushing the pink curves of her cheeks.

Verney, however, was as fair as she was dark and as boisterous as she was quiet. He was forever in mischief, with cut knees and dirty hands, but he was not really naughty and everybody who knew them loved them both equally.

Joseph Quizzit worked hard to make a living for his little family and had to provide plenty of food for his animals, for he was a humane man and never intentionally made any animal suffer. He worried about their lack of freedom and took great trouble to provide them all with whatever food was most natural for them. When he parted from them, he tried always to make certain that the customer who bought them would give them a good home. He had even been known to buy back, for a higher price, a monkey that he had heard was being teased by the grandchild of its new owner. Taken altogether, he was a very good man. He had his faults, as indeed had his animals, and he sometimes shouted at Silas or at the more mischievous of his stock. But in his heart of hearts he really hated constricting their movements and dreamed of being able to retire and move to the country, where he would buy a farm and where the animals could go free. It was with this secret aim in view that he worked so hard for such long hours and that he let Theodosia and Verney help him also.

At the time when these events took place, the Quizzits' shop was very full. In the center of the shop were piled cages full of birds. At the top were small cages of canaries and finches; then came larger cages in which there were several birds, pairs of lovebirds, harlequin-colored starlings chattering for all they were worth; flights of mynas who seemed to talk, so human were their cries; bright parakeets with crimson bills; and an unruly mob of sparrows quarreling their life away in a big cage to themselves. Lower down were rose-breasted parrots and lemon-crested cockatoos; and a cage out of whose darkness shone the blinking saucer eyes of a family of little owls, who flew from perch to perch on silent velvet wings uttering mournful cries all day. Two vivid blue macaws with long tails arched their beaks, opening and shutting them with dry raspings of their blunt tongues. Their sharp eyes, surrounded by white chalky baldness, winked as they laughed derisively at the owls. The odd-shaped holes and corners of this Tower of Babel were filled with cages of gray parrots who talked and chuntered away to themselves like senile old men, making weird cracking noises with their beaks, and high-pitched creaks by way of punctuation.

The two sides of the shop were covered with a stack of hutches and cages of all sizes and shapes housing a motley collection of animals. In the draft by the door of the shop was a bin for corn and another for split peas and beans. By the door to Arabella Quizzit's kitchen–living room stood a huge moated castle made of wood, complete with drawbridge and model cannon. In this lived a colony of white mice, who snuffled up and down its battlements and in and out of its gun turrets, deciding which was their best way out, only to be met, whichever way they turned, by the waters of the moat. They clung in rows to the top of the bars, presenting their white bellies and pink feet to the spectator, for all the world like prisoners in the dungeon of a medieval castle, pleading for release. But the squirrels in the next cage were always merry and bright. Never did they stop being busy, fetching and carrying nuts from one end of their cage to the other, sitting eating from their front paws, with their big plumed tails fluffed out in an S shape behind them. Now and again one would hop into the wheel that was provided for them to exercise on, and would run around and around for a bit, only to return to carrying nuts, chattering with more gusto than ever. Their neighbor was a raccoon.

This raccoon was, in a measure, tame. He was sometimes allowed his partial liberty in the shop on a long chain. He was a good scavenger and would eat any odd bits of meat left by the other animals, washing each piece in a puddle of water in the most careful manner. He hated children and if put outside the front of the shop in the summer he would snarl and snap angrily at passing babies, especially if they happened to be crying. He had a white face with black hair around his eyes, like spectacles, and his naked paws protruded from the rest of his fur, so that he looked like someone wearing a fur coat but with bare hands and feet. He was very cunning. There was a tank of crabs in the shop in which he would fish with his tail. When a crab gripped his tail with its nippers out, he would snatch it, and taking care to get the crab sideways into his mouth, he would greedily devour it. Sometimes he made a sly grab into a cage full of small birds and popped one of them into his greedy mouth, but when he did this he had to be put back into his cage until Mr. Quizzit was once more in a good temper and again gave him his freedom.

On the floor below the raccoon was a porcupine whose dry quills rustled like the wind through bamboo thickets. He was a very good-tempered fellow, but when his patience was exhausted by the continual teasing of the raccoon, he would dart a quiver full of spines up at him. Mr. Quizzit kept this porcupine not to sell but in the hope that when it died a natural death he would cut it open and find in its stomach a sort of stone called a bezoar, about which he had read in an old book on medicine. A bezoar was said to be worth as much as five hundred crowns, for when it was ground up and mixed with certain medicines it was supposed to have all sorts of virtues and powers of healing.

Then there was a box full of jerboas with their docile eyes and long thick-ended tails. They hopped, like boxers in the cold, on long hind legs, with their short front ones folded up in front of them, their sharp yellow teeth bared in an incessant grin. With plaintive feeble cries they hopped to and fro, dragging their tails through the sawdust in a crisscross pattern of arcs. Their ears were covered with a network of red veins and were so thin that you could see the light of a candle flame through them.

Some of the monkeys that lived on this wall looked as if they were children who had got inside an empty monkey skin. They smiled, then wiped their smiles away with little gray hands, and then smiled again. They ate their fruit delicately and with great care, spitting each pip out upon the floor. In the main they were happy and laughed or cried as the mood seized them.

The armadillo was very friendly but spent a great deal of his time hidden away in his bedroom wrapped up in his impenetrable armor like a knobbly cannon ball. Above him was a cote full of doves who with their contented chorus of cool-rool, cool-rool soothed him to sleep all day long. A coop of quarrelsome gamecocks with golden arching tails and flaming breasts stood alongside. They, however, were excessively irritated by the noise made by the doves and in consequence were even more quarrelsome. Above them were a lot of cavies—so many you couldn't count them—and even more rabbits. Blue rabbits, black rabbits, rabbits with straight ears, rabbits with lop ears, white rabbits with chocolate-colored ears and chocolate boots, big rabbits, little rabbits. In fact, rabbits to suit all tastes.

A species of beastly, naked rat inhabited another cage. No one would buy them, they looked so unpleasant, and as they increased at a prodigious rate, Mr. Quizzit was at his wits' end to know what to do with them.

A crested hoopoe lived next door to a cage full of soft-voiced ouzels.

At the back of the shop there were rows of shelves. On the top shelf there were a pair of hares. Alongside was a cage full of bats, all hanging upside down, wrapped tight in their leathery wings, never showing any sign of life all day. And beside them was a box of rooks who cawed without stopping, opening their beaks wide to reveal hungry red gorges. Below these, on one long shelf, were three fox cubs. They were shy and stayed curled up most of the time, their pointed noses covered by bushy tails, their brilliant eyes observing, and their sharp ears listening to everything. The next shelf was divided in two. One half was made into a box with a piece of glass, and inside it was a dead branch on which wound an almost invisible snake. The other half contained a glass box, half water and half island, in which lived a variety of toad called a Surinam toad.

On the bottom shelf was an assortment of boxes, cages, and canisters in which customers could carry away their purchases.

In the rounded portion of the shop formed by the bow window, the most expensive and interesting animals and fish were displayed to the public. In the middle was the most spectacular exhibit from the whole of Mr. Quizzit's collection, that unusual and almost extinct bird, the dodo. The one that was until a short time ago to be seen, stuffed, along with the funeral effigies of the English monarchs in waxwork at Westminster Abbey was in fact reputed to be this very one. He was very, very old and had been in Mr. Quizzit's family for as long as he could remember. He, of course, was not for sale, but was regarded as the talisman or cornerstone of the whole business. Hence his having the place of honor in the center of the bay window.

This old gentleman (for he was thought to be a cock bird, as he had never shown any signs of becoming broody or of laying an egg) presented a very venerable appearance. He was low in stature, about the size of a swan, and stood upon short thick

yellow legs clad in feathers to the knees. His plumage was
grizzled blue-gray in color but must have once been black. His
wings, which were too small to render a bird of such bulk any
use as flying organs, together with his tail, were of the color and
dustiness of old parchment. His head, which was very large for
the rest of his body, was ornamented with nothing but a huge
beak. The smooth shape of his head reminded one of the tonsure
of a monk, with much the same reverent appearance. But the
rest of his face, especially around his beak and yellow eye, was
naked and scurfy as if it were moldering away with age. The top
half of his beak bore a resemblance to that of a parrot but was
much more hooked. His nostrils were large and gaping, his
whole beak was black and shiny except for a blotch of red
above the hook. Two bony ridges just where his beak joined his
head gave his whole face a strange wrinkled appearance.

This dodo hardly ate anything; the Quizzits had never heard
him utter a sound and he scarcely ever moved. His only exertion
was to flex his toes and to blink his eyes. Now and again, with a
puff he blew out his feathers so that they stood on end all over
his body. Then with a sigh he let them fall slowly back into
place, again very gently settling one upon another. But he
seemed to watch everything and everybody. The Quizzits regarded him with an awe almost amounting to reverence. They
consulted his silent shape as an oracle. They thought him excep-
tionally wise, even though it is commonly believed that the
reason these birds became extinct was that, being so stupid and
inquisitive, they allowed themselves to be slaughtered indiscrimi-

nately while they innocently watched their killers advancing upon them. It is said that their breasts have a fine flavor and quality, two or three of which if made into a pie furnish enough food to feed a large company.

On one occasion the poor old bird was seen to be moist-eyed and Mr. Quizzit, suspecting an attack of the rheum, instructed Theodosia and Verney to wrap the patient in a warm gray woolen shawl and stand an earthenware hot-water bottle at his feet while they sat on each side of him encouraging him to partake of warm posset. But the dodo was simply crying for the lack of other dodo companionship and sat there, the tears streaming down his beak, looking for all the world like a big ball of gray knitting wool, until the two Quizzit children began howling in sympathy so that their father had to send them back upstairs and leave the dodo to recover in his own good time.

Behind the dodo stood a large branch planted in a tub of moist sand, swathed in a tent of the finest and most transparent muslin Mrs. Quizzit could obtain. Inside this there lived and bred large numbers of caterpillars, all provided with their favorite leaves. Each in his turn, following the course of nature, turned from caterpillar into chrysalis and then in due course into the fully formed butterfly. They lived without enmity and were altogether a very happy colony, with beetles living at their feet that unwittingly provided the birds with food.

Behind the caterpillars' tent, on a stand, stood a large glass tank or aquarium full of angelfish, golden carp, striped zebra fish, and frail transparent creatures called sea horses who seemed to have no thickness at all and who clung by their tails to the weeds that grew there.

At each corner of the window there stood two more special animals, on one side an extremely doleful ape and on the other a very merry-looking brown bear. Neither of them was in a cage but both were chained by collars to two posts that were fixed to the floor. The dodo of course was not in a cage, he was entirely free.

The ape, who was perhaps the most unhappy beast in the shop, had a very flat face, olive-brown hair, naked pink hands, and was destitute of a tail. The bear, who came from the steppes of Russia, always seemed to be smiling. He, like the ape, stood upright, but by his good spirits he gave the passersby every encouragement to enter the shop, for he cast such glances of amusement over his shoulder that people thought there must be something interesting to see behind him.

These then were the inhabitants of Mr. Quizzit's shop. A motley crew of birds, beasts, and fishes living together in the utmost harmony, in the closest proximity, and with very little disagreement. However the noise was deafening, for everyone sang, cried, talked, laughed, shouted, growled, or whistled in his or her particular way all day, but at night—ah! well, at night we shall see what happened.

When Silas put up the shutters every night and retired to his loft, and when Mr. and Mrs. Quizzit were safe in their four-poster at the top of the house, and the children snored in their truckle beds, a strange transformation took place. For a moment, everyone, unaccustomed to the darkness, was silent, but then the bear, the dodo, and the ape all revolved together like wax-works and faced into the shop instead of into the shuttered windows. Then, at a slight almost imperceptible sign from the dodo, everyone began talking again—but this time not in a dozen unintelligible tongues. In the dusk, from under each pair of gleaming eyes, there came voices that all spoke in the same language, English—which was understood, if not spoken, by all—so that conversation was even more animated than during the daytime. So animated and so noisy in fact that the dodo, who was their natural, unopposed leader, was afraid they would wake Mr. Quizzit, who would do something drastic to stop them talking and disturbing his family's rest.

It was decided therefore that for a week seven of the animals should take it in turn to tell the rest of the company a strange and fascinating story. The raccoon was very eager and so it was agreed that he should start the storytelling. The dodo, being the oldest, as always appointed himself chairman. It was hoped that after a week of comparative silence the animals would learn to keep quiet or that the Quizzits would have got into such a habit of deep sleep that nothing short of a fire would wake them.

Our story really begins on the first night of this experiment when the raccoon began to tell his story in a high, sharp voice.

## Chapter II

# NIGHT THE FIRST . . . MONDAY
# . . . THE RACCOON'S TALE

*M INE* is a story of revenge," started the raccoon, licking his lips and rolling his eyes malevolently. "As you know, I once escaped from this shop," he went on in a sly voice, "and I intend to escape again, but this time I shall not allow myself to be brought back so easily, you can depend on it. The first time I escaped it was for a reason. You may remember a tall surly man called Quilt who had young Silas' job before he came here. Well, it was to get my revenge upon him that I escaped the last time.

"He had been persistently cruel to all of us, as you who were here at that time will remember, impatient, sharp, and particularly nasty to me, keeping me on short commons, finally making me really hate him by tying my tail to the bars of my cage so that I could not turn around in it, until Esmerelda the monkey managed, hours afterwards, to lean far out of her cage and undo it for me. I vowed then that I would get back at him sooner or later and I will again too when I next escape, for it was his fault that I was recaptured the last time.

"Soon after Mr. Quizzit dismissed him, when he found he was selling the straw that should have been our bedding, I saw my opportunity of escape. Silas, who was new then, had left open the door from the shop to the parlor, and beyond that the back door into the yard stood open also, with the sunshine pouring in across the threshold inviting one to run out of doors without more ado. So as I had that day been given the freedom of the shop and was hampered only by my short chain, I darted across the parlor without Arabella, who was leaning over the stove noisily stirring a saucepan, seeing me. In the twinkling of an eye, I was up the apple tree, onto the next wall from an overhanging branch, down into the warehouse yard next door, from there up onto the roof, and six or seven chimney stacks, away before Silas had discovered my absence.

"I heard them raising a hue and cry, and peeping out could see Silas, Quizzit, and Arabella searching high and low crying, 'Animal escaped, fierce animal loose, raccoon escaped. Stop him someone, stop him!' They roused the whole street. The butcher with his knife and steel clanking at his blue striped apron, the baker with his white hat, and the candlestick maker with his tallow-spotted apron all ran out of their shops brandishing the tools of their trade, supported by their wives and apprentices in a great state of alarm. They chased up and down for a bit, but no one thought of looking higher than their noses, so I remained hidden by my chimney pot, resolving to stay there until nightfall and then make my way to the place where I had heard from a white rat that Quilt worked.

"Then it grew dark, and as the light disappeared, I descended from my vantage point and strolled down the street to see what was happening. In front of Mr. Quizzit's shop I read a notice that said: 'Lost one dangerous raccoon; reward 5 guineas: Take care as he is very spiteful, especially to children.' I had no idea that I was worth so much but I don't think anyone could call me spiteful; I just don't like screaming brats, that's all.

"On I went down the street; all was quiet, I could hear the watchman calling the hours several streets off. 'Two o'clock and a fine frosty night,' he called. So it *was* frosty. My feet very nearly stuck to the pavement it was so cold. I thought to myself that I must find a warm bed for the rest of the night or I should freeze to death. After traversing several streets, I found a house in front of which the frost had melted from the pavement. Taking a quick look in either direction to see what was afoot, I slipped through the railings and down the area steps. Finding a corner over a warm grating, I curled myself up and fell asleep.

"In the morning I found it was the basement of a turkish bath where the fashionable beaux subjected themselves to the discomfort of hot steam baths in order to reduce their weight. I didn't get a very long night's sleep for as soon as it first began to get light I was forced to move on.

"I knew that Master Quilt had gone to work at a grocer's when he left the animal shop. I made my way to this establishment and, creeping into a small pantry window that I found open on the ground floor—I may say devouring a brace of partridge and a game pie on my way through—climbed to the top of the house, clanking my abominable chain behind me, where I thought I should find my enemy sleeping.

"But each room I crept into contained other nightcaps than his, which I knew to be a red flowered one with a white bobble, but nowhere was it to be seen. As I stood at the door of the last bedroom I could hear the rest of the household stirring beneath me, and I thought it was high time I made myself scarce. I repaired to the yard where I found a miserable skulking yellow cur, cowering in a kennel.

" 'Tell me, you wretch, where the man Quilt has gone to work, or I will devour every inch of you, ears and claws and all.' At once the groveling beast blurted out that Quilt had left three weeks before and had gone to work as a doorman at a certain 'Academy for Young Ladies' in Jermyn Street.

"The day had not quite dawned and I was still able to get from the Strand to Jermyn Street by way of the rooftops without descending to street level more than half a dozen times. When I did finally get there, I just had time to slip down the chimney of Miss Fossle's Academy for Young Ladies and to conceal myself in a strange box of ropes and chains on the wall in her best salon. It was here, it turned out, that the young ladies were taught how to look more young and how to be more ladylike.

"I had not been asleep very long in my hiding place before I heard the high-pitched cackle of lots of females arriving. These were Miss Fossle and her pupils. Her Academy existed for that type of woman who is either too old or too stupid to be considered attractive by other people, so they expend all their time, energies, and feeble brain power on trying to be what they are not and can never be. They soon entered the room after I had heard their voices approaching, and began to perform all sorts of pranks.

"Miss Fossle, who was a huge woman well past sixty, dressed in pale blue and wearing ostrich feathers in her hair, although it was scarcely past eleven o'clock in the morning, was taking a class in deportment. She stalked up and down the room, a large leather-bound volume balanced carefully, so as not to damage her feathers, on the crown of her head.

"One of her assistants was stretching her pupils out flat on a board and making them breathe with a whole encyclopedia balanced on their diaphragms. In another corner a retired, be-whiskered dragoon was teaching a whole squad of young admiring women the secrets of a true military carriage, and a few passé old beaux were mincing their way through a minuet with some of the most shriveled spinsters for partners that you could ever behold.

"An elderly harridan with a hooked nose, and wearing clothes that would have suited a girl a quarter her age, was in the act of taking snuff, while her daughter was having a sort of broad leather band fixed under her chin and over her head. To the top of this by means of a loop was attached a gigantic iron hook, which in its turn was set in a large block and pulley; this was hung from the ceiling, and the ropes and chain that operated this piece of mechanism (which I found out afterwards were for stretching the necks of those vain creatures who wished to be swan-necked) were housed in my box.

"They had no sooner got the band fixed, when a footman came up to my box and started to hand out a chain that very soon payed out by the side of me. Having pulled this young woman off her feet, she hung suspended as if from a gallows, straight and stiff with her arms to her sides. He then returned to the middle of the room and fixed another stout young woman, who was so tightly waisted she could scarcely breathe, into her noose; coming over to the box again, he laid hold of my chain, which hung from it, and gave it an almighty wrench, swinging me out of the box and into the middle of the dancing spinsters and their beaux.

"What a scene of confusion ensued! Everyone screamed, girls and women stampeded, while the dragoon cut at me with his sword, endangering all the legs of the young ladies under whose skirts I tried to conceal myself. Plaster casts, harpsichord stool, vases of flowers, tambourines, all went flying, breaking and splintering as they fell. So great was the screaming that a whole room full of young seamstresses from the floor above ran in to see what was about, but seeing me dashing hither and thither, only joined in the fun, adding their screams to those of Miss Fossle's young ladies.

"The snuff-taking mother demanded that her suspended daughter should be allowed to descend, although she was quite safe from any attacks that they seemed to expect me to make. After several darts in the direction of the door that the seamstresses had left open, I managed to slip away, down the stairs and out into the back courtyard.

"Here I met a rat who had come out to see what all the noise was about. Seeing me, he stopped in his tracks and politely asked if he could be of any service to me. To which I replied that he could as I was looking for a man named Quilt whom, I had understood from a grocer's cur, was working as porter in Miss Fossle's Academy. The rat said that he knew him well for he had only seen him a day or two before entering the back door of a taxidermist's not far from the Albany, in whose yard he was wont to scavenge, as there were always plenty of scraps there for his rat family.

"Off I went by the back yards between Curzon Street and the Albany, only meeting a few cats and scaring a scullery maid or two, until I came to one that by its fetid smell and the sight of several boards on which were stretched skins nailed out to dry in the sun, I knew to be the taxidermist's. Seeing no one about, I popped in at the back door and just had time to leap up onto a shelf among a row of stuffed animals, when the shopkeeper entered with a customer whom he had met in the street.

"They walked into the shop while the nearsighted old taxidermist pointed out his wares, trying with all the persuasion he could muster to get his customer to buy something. But he did not seem inclined until he came to me, when they both stopped and looked at me very closely. The shopkeeper, who couldn't for the moment remember stuffing me, said, 'I shouldn't like you to have that model, sir; it is not very lifelike, not well posed and the eyes are bad—I could not get the best quality, they are only second best. Wouldn't you prefer this other one, sir,' pointing to a moth-eaten otter that was ridiculously posed with an artificial fish between its jaws on artificial slippery rocks surrounded by artificial grass.

"But the customer was determined to have me and said so as he observed my fur closely through his glass. The shopman, who was doing a quick reckoning in his head as to how much he should charge for me, flicked me with a duster and started to try and lift me down.

"But here I thought it was high time that I made myself scarce, so with one leap out of the hands of the astonished old man, I was out of the shop, up a tree, and onto the roof of the next-door shop, only to find myself face to face with a jackdaw who sat on a nest in the corner made by a chimney and the roof.

"So surprised were we both that neither said a word for a moment, until she opened her beak and let forth a great squawk. 'Silence, or I will bite your head off,' I snarled in the most menacing voice I could manage. More terrified than ever and scarcely able to breathe with fright, the poor thing begged for mercy. 'I will spare you on one slender chance,' I said, 'and that is if you can tell me the whereabouts of one Quilt who used to work in this taxidermist's shop beneath us.'

" 'Ah, yes,' she gasped, 'I can and will if you will take your

heavy paw off my neck so that I can breathe. He is a footman at
My Lord Chief Justice's house in Piccadilly. I know for I saw
him this morning with my own eyes—in fact he threw a stone at
me as I was gathering sticks for my nest in the Justice's garden
this very hour.'

"Thanking her and telling her in no uncertain terms that if she
was telling me a lie I would return and gobble her up, eggs, nest
and all, I left her in a flutter of feathers and consternation.

"Halfway down Piccadilly I found the house to which the
daw had directed me. A boot boy was cleaning a whole battery
of shoes and boots by the back door, and the front door was
flanked by two imposing porters in a green and yellow livery,
with white powdered wigs upon their heads, holding themselves
very erect. So it was no use trying to make an entrance by either
of those two ways. But fortunately I found an attic bedroom
window open, belonging to one of the kitchen maids who, fresh
from the country, liked the air to blow into her room even if it
was laden with soot instead of the scent of buttercups and hay.

"In I went and started on my voyage of exploration. It was a
big house, and by the time I had looked into all the rooms on the
top floors without success it was past noon.

"I was just entering a little anteroom next to the Lord Chief
Justice's bedroom, when I heard approaching voices. Just in time
I leaped onto the top of a wardrobe and from there I sprang
upon the chandelier, all glass drops and lusters, where I commanded a fine view of what was going on. Four footmen were in
the center of the carpet, another carried a pile of hot towels,

another carried two large jugs of cold water, and his partner two steaming jugs of hot water. They poured the contents of their jugs into the bath, the one with the towels stationed himself behind it, while a very dignified liveried servant entered and felt the heat of the water with the tips of his fingers. Pronouncing it to be just right, he retired to His Lordship's bedroom to announce that his bath was waiting. With a bad-tempered growl, His Lordship rolled out of bed and soon entered the room wearing a woolen nightcap and almost supported by the stiff folds of a thick padded dressing gown. He was a large red-faced man with an expression like a thundercloud, and it appeared that being called in the morning did not improve his temper. Throwing off his dressing gown and nightshirt, he stepped into the hip bath, still wearing his nightcap. Letting out a yell like a jackal, he complained that it was too hot, then when they added more water it was too cold. At last all was well, and he bellowed for his breakfast.

"In a few minutes the door opened and who should walk in, resplendent in his master's livery carrying before him a silver tray laden with coffee, rolls, and boiled eggs, but Mr. Quilt, my sworn foe. At last my opportunity had arrived!

"I waited until he stood by My Lord's bath directly under my chandelier, and then plop! I fell straight as a plummet upon his periwigged head, and sank my teeth into his right ear. With a shriek of terror, he let go the tray, pouring a stream of scalding coffee and another of boiling milk down the naked back of his master, who with a roar like a lion leaped from his bath brandishing a long-handled brush with which he flailed about haphaz-

ardly at anything that was in his way. All the time the Judge
was splashing about in puddles of water all over the carpet
without a stitch on except his nightcap, and blinded by the
soapsuds that had gone into his eye. The attendant footmen
pranced around behind him dodging the blows he was dealing
with his brush, trying at the same time to hide their mirth and to
calm him down. Neither the Judge because of his temper, nor
Quilt because of his deceitful nature, were very much liked and
they were all rather pleased to watch their discomfort.

"Quilt roared even louder than his master and swore terribly
at me, all the time tugging at my chain, but I only hung on the
harder and my teeth met through his ear, making him roar
louder than ever. The whole of the Brussels carpet was splashed
with water. In pools of milk and coffee floated sodden rolls, pats
of butter gently dissolving among them. Brown and white lakes
covered the rose and lily pattern of the carpet. Sugar and
strawberry preserve were mingled in an awful slide that ended in
a morass on the floorboards by the fireplace.

"The rest of the household staff—the butler, the housekeeper,
the cook, the still-room maids—all the servants, rushed to see
what terrible calamity had happened to produce such a row.
Throwing open the door of the Judge's chamber, the housekeeper swooned, the butler was speechless, the still-room maids
burst out giggling at the sight of their naked master, and the
cook began belaboring me with a wooden spoon, as she happened to be keeping company with Quilt and was the only one
who liked him. But I only held on harder still.

" 'Get out of here, all of you,' bellowed the Judge, clutching a towel around his waist. 'And take that infernal animal with you. Quilt, you are dismissed, get out I say, get out!' he positively screamed. Quilt had no option but to carry me with him for I refused to let go. With the entire staff giving both Quilt and me blows with every conceivable sort of weapon, we descended the staircase in a shouting mob, through the kitchen and out into the yard. All the time one of the footmen, who hated Quilt, had hold of my chain and kept giving it vicious tugs that each time tore at Quilt's ear as I held on like grim death.

"In the yard someone picked up a bucket of icy water and flung it full tilt over Quilt's head with me still stuck fast to his ear. But this had the effect they wanted, for the shock of the cold water made me gasp for breath, and with one last heave, the footman dragged me clear.

"The last I saw as I was crammed into a wicker basket was Quilt standing with bleeding ear, surrounded by a laughing circle of servants, his beautiful new livery dripping with water and beginning to shrink fast, so that his cuffs were working their way up his arms and his breeches up his thighs, while his cravat clutched his throat.

"The footman who had been so unremitting in his attentions on my chain had the day before seen Quizzit's notice of a reward and so, while the hullaballoo was still at its height, he slipped on his greatcoat and went off as fast as he could with my hamper to claim the five guineas.

"And that is how I was brought back to this accursed shop, very wet, tired, and hungry, but happy that I had been revenged on the monster Quilt. But I shall not be here much longer, for I am determined to effect my escape next time I am given the run of the shop, and it is for that reason that I am making myself so pleasant to Silas and the Quizzits. But once away this time I shall not return; at any rate, if I do, it will be as a dead raccoon you will see me and not as a live one."

"Bravo! Bravo!" cried all the animals and birds together. "A capital tale, a capital tale."

"I wonder if it is true," said one rose-tailed parrot to a lemon-crested cockatoo. "I care not," said he, "for it was capital entertainment for one night, capital entertainment, and I doubt if you could do better yourself."

"Oh, couldn't I?" said the parrot, on his mettle at once. "You wait. We will see tomorrow night whether I can or no."

Now this parrot was the only creature in the shop, except for a very old myna bird, who could not talk fluently at all times in English. The old myna spoke excellent Hindustani but his English came out very croakily, and with an Indian accent, so that he was rather shy of using it. But the parrot was not at all shy and used to hold quiet conversations with Theodosia and Verney when they were feeding him sunflower seeds or super-intending his bath.

On the day after the raccoon's tale had been narrated, at about five o'clock, just as the corners of the shop were beginning to become dark and mysterious with the approach of the night, Theodosia and Verney Quizzit happened to be feeding a sick guinea pig that occupied a cage just by the parrot's perch. As they bent over the little invalid, who was perfectly tame and had almost got over its temporary malady, they heard the parrot speak in his cracked little old voice:

"If you two little Quizzits want to hear a good yarn tonight, creep down the stairs and listen at the door after everyone is in bed. I'll warrant you'll hear something to keep you awake."

Theodosia and Verney looked at one another with surprise and nodded their assent, pleased but half afraid of their unexpected secret.

## Chapter III

# NIGHT THE SECOND . . . TUESDAY
# . . . THE PARROT'S TALE

*T*O the surprise of their parents, Theodosia and Verney went to bed early. Their hearts were aflutter, wondering if they would be able to stay awake and what it was they were going to hear. They lay pinching one another under the coverlets and humming to themselves, trying as hard as they could to stay awake. But it was of no avail, and as sure as night follows day, they were as sound asleep as usual when Arabella Quizzit peeped in on them on her way to bed.

Down below, however, the parrot began his tale, disappointed not to have his two human listeners but not so much so that he was prevented from telling his story.

"My tale isn't of petty revenge," began the parrot, scornfully cocking an eye at the raccoon, who merely smiled at him grudgingly and licked his chops, "but of piracy on the grand scale by broad daylight. Not that I hold with it, mind ye," he added hastily as he noticed some of his audience looking rather scandalized, in particular a lemon and green parakeet to whom he was rather partial, who distinctly shuddered. "But I was taken prisoner, as you might say, in a manner of speaking, if you get my meaning," he added, all of a fluster at the sight of the little parakeet's disapproval. However, when he saw that she had recovered, he went on.

"I first belonged to a young English sailor called Teggle, who had been press-ganged in the dark alleys of Yarmouth. He had me off an Italian sailor who couldn't pay his card debts in Naples; the Italian had me from an Arab who had carried his baggage once into Tunis, and he had stolen me from an ebony African who had trapped me in a net in his kraal with a bait of ripe figs. I sailed before the mast with my young sailor pal for three years, and then our ship, the *Pride of Lammermoor*, was taken prisoner in a bloody encounter off the coast of Madagascar by a pirate vessel captained by a rascally Moor named Il Tabaro. This Moorish buccaneer was the terror of the seven seas. His ship, the *Beatrice Maud*, had been an English vessel captured in the Bay of Biscay, and ever since had sailed the black flag of the skull and crossbones. Many terrible sights have I seen on those blood-stained decks—strap me if I haven't," croaked the parrot, suddenly becoming nautical in his language.

"What is a pirate like, pray tell us," whispered his little parakeet shyly.

"This one," said the parrot, "had a tawny complexion as dark as a walnut. A terrible livid scar gashed the blackness of his face from his ear to his shoulder blade, where with his cutlass the

captain of a French privateer had wounded him. He had wonderful white teeth that were so strong he could bite a piece of
thick rope in two; he wore his own hair braided in a short waxed
pigtail at the nape of his neck; he was a weatherbeaten man,
having lost his left eye in one scuffle, an arm in another, and a leg
in another. His trunk, however, was by no means lifeless, he
could still board a vessel and slash about him with his cutlass like
the best of 'em. His great ears were drawn down unnaturally by
heavy gold earrings, and his one remaining hand was smothered
in rings that he had filched from many a dead or living hand.

"I saw him once command a captive to hand over his valu-
ables—this man, thinking to outwit him, swallowed one of his
best rings, but if you get my meaning, Il Tabaro's dagger didn't
let it stay inside him for long. On the stump of his arm he wore a
wooden block, nicely turned like the leg of a table, with a socket
in it. Into this he screwed whatever he needed, be it knife, fork,
spoon, or even telescope, but when none of these were needed
he had an evil white ivory hand with jointed fingers and thumb
that had been made for him by a clever craftsman in Chinese
waters. In the clenched fingers of this hand he always carried a
lace handkerchief heavily perfumed, for strangely enough he
was a particular man, with quite cultivated habits. In place of his
missing leg he wore a thick wooden rod, worn and polished with
use, on which he cut notches to note the number of throats his
dagger had cut.

"Il Tabaro's dagger was small, but although it had a jeweled
scabbard and a pearl handle, it was wickedly sharp—woe betide

anyone who crossed him, for he was quick to draw it out and quick to use it. He dressed carefully and well. As he always had the pick of the clothes aboard each ship they took, he had a rich and extensive wardrobe. Embroidered coats, lace cuffs, flowered waistcoats, silken hose, doeskin breeches, silver shoe buckles, feathered hats, carved walking sticks, he wore them all; a dandy he certainly was with his rich perfumes and jewels of every sort, even ropes of pearls if he had a mind to it.

"After he had captured us, we were herded into the bows of our ship with our hands tied behind us and gags over our mouths—at least the sailors were. I wasn't, but I clung to young Teggle's shoulder through thick and thin; I even had my tail feathers chopped off with a slice from a cutlass. When we were all crowded together, they started to lay waste the vessel. We had been carrying a cargo of silks, spices, carpets, and coffee from the East, and we were loaded as heavily as could be, despite the fact that when Il Tabaro gave chase we had thrown overboard half our cargo of coffee in an endeavor to escape. His men carted up the great brass-bound coffers containing the spices, now and again bursting one open and spilling the contents about the decks, perfuming the sea breezes with aromatic odors of the East. Bales of cotton and rolls of silk were wantonly cut into, many a corsair strutted up and down proudly wrapped in a toga of the finest Chinese silk over his bloodstained garments. Our fine Persian and Indian carpets were spread on the deck of the *Beatrice Maud*, while her crew stamped up and down on them barefooted, spilling wine and spices on the

priceless patterns. Silk and rigging trailed into the water from
the decks of the defeated vessel, while sharks and scavenger fish
swooped and dived rivaling each other in their ferocity to snap
at whatever chanced to be swept overboard.

"When they had finished unloading our ship, they then proceeded to cut down all that remained of her rigging, threw
overboard her anchor and chain, lopped off her three masts at
the deck, hacked away her steering wheel, and removed all her
pieces of cannon, until she was but a bare floating hulk, with
nothing on board but food and water for a handful of wounded
and broken human beings. Then taking us in tow, they returned
to their own ship, from which we heard sounds of drunken
carousal the whole night through. Although they did not untie
our hands, they did remove our gags so that we could at least
talk, and one of our number who was unwounded had his hands
manacled behind him in such a way that he was able, with my
help, to feed the others with the food the pirates had left us. But
he was quite unable to free the hands of his companions, nor
was my beak strong enough to peck through their bonds.

"While we were towed behind our conqueror for some
leagues, we were forced to be the unwilling witnesses of the
attack on another vessel, which Il Tabaro treated in the same
way as he had served ours, putting them also in tow behind us.
We observed him commanding his men to burn and pillage a
native island in the Pacific, where he had to stop for supplies of
fresh water and fruit, as these were running low on all three
vessels, although there seemed to be an abundance of wine and

grog on the *Beatrice Maud*. When within two or three days' sail of this island that he had wiped out, we sighted another island several miles distant from our port bow. Applying a glass to his eye, our mate of the half-free hands described what he said seemed to be ragged figures on it. We were at that time going through a part of the sea fraught with dangerous eddies and currents—whirlpools sucked under any piece of wood thrown overboard like the hungry maw of a beast—and Il Tabaro was finding it difficult to sail with our two dismasted vessels in procession behind him, but he appeared to know the route and to be making, in some devilish way, for the island we had sighted. Soon it was dark and, as there was no moon, we could see no more. We were forced to give up trying to find out where he was taking us, for we had no doubt that he was going to abandon all of us on some lonely reef.

"But imagine our horror next morning when, on coming on deck, we found that we were within a stone's throw, not of an island made of earth and rocks and natural vegetation, but a most unusual island consisting entirely of crippled ships, like ourselves. On closer inspection the ragged shapes were indeed human beings running up and down the decks of their abandoned craft like monkeys.

"Suddenly one of our shipmates shouted out, 'It's the Sargasso Sea, me hearties, haven't ye heard tell of it? 'Tis made of floatin' weed and the hulks of lost ships.' What he said was true, for the sea was blocked with great masses of floating weed, like the nests of a gigantic seabird. We were being drawn nearer and nearer to this floating mortuary by the relentless eddies and currents that Il Tabaro knew so well; for he had cut both of us, his two latest victims, adrift and was now making sail to windward as fast as he could to escape being dragged into the terrible net of weeds formed by the floating water-logged island to which he had brought us. Soon our unfortunate ship, with its manacled company, was drawn in close to the outermost hulks, and we found ourselves grappled to it by floating tentacles of weed and rotting vegetation. In a moment the horde of ragged beings we had been observing were on our decks and clamoring at us in a dozen different tongues.

"They were a strange, motley, unkempt crew, bearded and long-haired, wearing clothes of an old-fashioned cut, much patched and darned. The women were as wild and dirty-looking a lot as the men, and there were even small children with hair as long as their parents'. They crowded around us in a shouting rabble, weeping and looking most pitifully at us. For we were soon made to understand by those who could speak a little English that they had thought we had come to rescue them, instead of which they found we had come to join them in their banishment on this floating island. Poor luckless castaways, they freed our hands and began to relate the story of their domain.

"They said that this was the Sargasso Sea indeed, that it kept its position pretty constantly and was so situated that, unless pilots knew the channels through the dangerous currents, it was impossible to come upon it except to end there as an accidental addition to this weed-woven land. From time to time, they told

43

us, Il Tabaro visited them, leaving behind a further shipload of unhappy mariners to add to their numbers. But how were we to live, we asked them, as they fell on the few kegs of ship's biscuits and water left by the corsair captain in the hold of our vessel. They explained that they collected rainwater, of which there was no lack, for that particular part of the ocean was wracked with terrible storms more often than favored with fine weather. During these storms, their crazy island, welded together by its putrifying mass of weed and rotten timber, seemed about to crack up and disintegrate, so fast did it revolve in the treacherous eddies. It became the roosting places for the great albatross, whose wingspan was the greatest of any bird, and whole flocks of seabirds herded into the very cabins that the people themselves inhabited.

"As to what they ate, fish they were able to catch in abundance, and seabirds when they got used to the fishy taste made them an oily stew. But of vegetables they had none, and fruit was in short supply. An occasional tree had taken root among the rotten plants and sand of some of the older boats—maybe the seed was dropped by some passing bird years before—and it was manured with fish and rotten weeds and encouraged to bear fruit, which fruit were carefully guarded by a trusted rota of guards and was apportioned out to the inhabitants. Fortunately they had discovered that a concoction made from a certain sort of weed that was in great abundance was very good as a substitute for green vegetables. It was very unpleasant, but they were forced to partake of it regularly lest they should all be carried off by an attack of the dread scurvy.

"Some of the people of this strange land had never seen the real world at all. For they had been born and brought up by their parents who had since died on the doomed raft. Now and again a vessel rotted so that its timbers sank into the sea, but the ever-encroaching weed quickly closed up the gap as if it were the door of a tomb. The age of some of the ships was not known, nor their country of origin. Spanish galleons rocked alongside Egyptian barges, the carved prow of some savage war boat rubbed the plain timbers of a Norseman's decks. Dhows, junks, and coracles were all neighbors; rough rafts of unhewn timber and the remains of Eskimos' skin boats lay helpless together side by side.

"The nationalities of the people who manned these boats varied to the same degree. Spaniards, Italians, Vikings, Africans, Chinese, every race and creed, lived here together in equal abandon, accepting each other's differences, each trying to understand the other's language and behavior. Few crimes were committed, indeed they were already virtually imprisoned forever. Few people were jealous of another man's lot for no man had more possessions than another. Life was hard, existence barely possible, yet soon our crew of lost souls found themselves fitting into this weird life as if they had been born to it. Few there were who had been of a philosophical turn of mind before, but now it had been forced on them or perish they surely must from madness.

"Now and again our boredom was relieved by the appearance of a spouting whale, or a fight between an octopus and a shark. Sometimes whole fleets of a strange inflated jellyfish, called

Portuguese men-of-war, were drawn into the awful suction that surrounded us; for this reason few wild creatures, except for winged ones, frequented the confines of our world.

"You will ask, as I can hear some of you already doing so," for here several of the animals had become particularly voluble and restless, "how I came to escape. Well, it was in this wise:

"One day Il Tabaro returned with more trophies, and it was then that young, or rather now middle-aged, Teggle saw a chance for my escape. Fixing a note to my leg, he launched me on the breeze and told me to fly into the nearest porthole of the *Beatrice Maud*, there to conceal myself. 'Then somehow, God knows how,' he said, 'try and make your way back to England by hopping from one ship to another as a stowaway.'

"Living in this way like a winged rat in the holds of countless ships, I eventually, many years afterwards, made my way by ship, land, and even wings to England. Bearing on my leg the witness of the horrors I and the others had gone through, I flew to the public house in Stepney kept by the wife and parents of young Teggle, where I found it still in existence doing a brisk trade. One foul Saturday night I arrived in the bar parlor, more dead than alive, sodden with fog and beaten by the wind. I was just able to struggle to the shoulder of my master's wife and see that she undid my message. With a shriek she swooned into the arms of a hearty fellow who stood serving ale and porter at her side. Fortunately on this night the bar was nearly empty and so few people knew of my mysterious arrival and the landlady's equally mysterious fainting fit, for she was healthy enough as a rule. The reason for her attack was that the hearty young man who had caught her in his arms had only the week before become her husband. Young Teggle's parents being dead, and he missing for more than ten years, she had thought it quite safe to assume herself a widow. However, the day after my arrival she went before a justice of the peace and made a clean breast of the whole thing.

"He was shown my salt-stained message and my battered plumage, and listened attentively to the whole story. At the conclusion of which, he laughed a loud laugh and dismissed the bewildered couple with instructions not to listen to such a seaman's yarn, laying the whole thing down to some malicious mischief of a jealous rival or the anonymous ravings of a madman. The former Mrs. Teggle and her new husband, who were only too glad to put such a complexion on it, left him rejoicing, and sold me to Mr. Quizzit, not liking to have such a reminder of young Teggle so constantly before them. So now you perceive, friends, how I came here, and I leave it to you to judge how wonderful my story is, every word of which, I swear to you on oath, is true."

"Well, that is a strange tale to be sure," said the animals in unison. Some of them, it is true, were inclined to agree with the magistrate. However, they had enjoyed their evening's entertainment, so they said no more. Looking forward eagerly to the next night when, it had been decided, the ape would tell her story, they all fell silent, some to doze and others to eat their way through the daylight hours.

## Chapter IV

# NIGHT THE THIRD . . . WEDNESDAY
# . . . THE APE'S TALE

*T*HE next day when Theodosia and Verney passed the parrot's perch looking a bit shamefaced, the old bird cried out, "Heave to, me hearties." And when they stopped beside him and gave him half of a ripe William pear, he went on in the utmost good humor, "And what befell ye last night, pray?"

"We couldn't stay awake," said Theodosia.

"We sang to keep ourselves awake," said Verney, "and pinched each other." The old parrot wagged his head from side to side as he bobbed up and down on his perch, rattling the chain that attached him to it, laughing quietly in Mr. Quizzit's own particular way. So droll did he appear to be that the children laughed aloud with him.

"I can soon remedy that," he said. "Take a handful of my sunflower seeds and sprinkle them in your bed. You won't go to sleep then. You'll be like the Princess with the pea under her mattress." They promised and declared they would do so, saying that they would creep down and sit on the bottom step of the stairs as soon as they heard their parents stop moving about.

That night when all was quiet, after their mother had peeped around the door to be deceived by their downcast lids, they slid out of bed, put on their flannel gowns and slippers, and crept to the head of the stairs. Here all was quiet except for the snores that issued regularly from Mr. Quizzit's gaping mouth and the whispering of the animals below. Stationed on the bottom stair, their arms around each other and the shop door just ajar, they were in time to hear the ape commence her story.

"It is I, who am in reality a Princess of the blood royal from a distant kingdom across the sea, who can tell the strangest story. For within this repellent twisted form of mine, there is housed the gentle nature and doubly bewitched spirit of one who was the most beautiful, kindhearted Princess this realm had ever known. But I will not harp so unsuitably on the qualities I was said to have possessed and have so sadly lost, but will tell you the story of how I exchanged my shape with that of the tame beast who was my constant companion when I trod the marble terraces of my father's palace as a free and happy girl.

"My ape, Clarissa, and I were the greatest friends. She had been caught by the royal huntsmen on the day of a great hunt held to celebrate my brother's coming of age. She was at that time so young that she still had to be fed by hand, and had never learned the fear of human beings that sooner or later we learn in such a hard school. When they brought her to my boudoir her wrinkled face and placid, deep eyes betokened an instant attachment to me. I at once fell quite in love with her, for she possessed such affectionate ways and performed the gayest antics.

"We became inseparable companions. In fact, she would scarcely ever leave me, sitting even by my bed at night clasping in her rough grip my own bejeweled fingers. She sat at my table dipping her bread in the same dish and drinking from the same goblet—eating her fruit with more delicacy and refinement than many of the court ladies. She attended me on my walks and even rode out with me, sitting on a specially made sidesaddle on a piebald pony.

"One midsummer day toward evening we went for a walk together in the palace grounds. Clarissa gathered a bunch of peacock feathers lost by the proud birds that thronged the gardens. Capering with delight, she held them first on her head, mocking the walk of one of my father's courtiers whom she disliked; then, holding them as a tail, she mimicked the mincing gait of the peacocks themselves. Running and walking by turns, happily tossing a ball between us, we wandered a long way from the palace to a corner of the park dense with trees and not much frequented. It was getting late, night was drawing on; and as neither of us liked the dark, we turned to retrace our steps toward home. Running in the half-light to catch the ball that Clarissa had thrown me, I tripped, catching my toe in a hole under the projecting root of a great oak tree. To my surprise and no small fright, a thin, angry little voice cried out, 'A curse on you, you clumsy mortal, look what you have done.'"

"Clarissa bounded to my side and together we went down on our knees in the moss to investigate the hole. There we saw a strange sight. I had stubbed my toe on the house of one of the fairy craftsmen who fashion glasses for Titania, the Queen of the Fairies. In one second I had shattered the whole stock of glassware that the little old man had been at such pains to make. He had, at that moment, been putting the finishing touches to a glass goblet of such intricacy and delicate proportions that the like of it had never been seen before. There it lay broken to bits among the moss and oak apples. The little man's wrath, perhaps because of his size, was quite terrifying. He stamped up and down cursing and tearing his beard out by the roots, and nothing I could do would appease him. Clarissa looked on wide-eyed, spellbound, for she knew then, as we the wild things of the forest know, how terrible can be the rage and revenge of a spiteful fairy if one has the misfortune to cross one.

"Suddenly his rage reached fever pitch and, darting me a piercing look from his tiny little eyes, he shouted, 'Curse you for an infernal, meddling mortal. May your clumsy feet be turned to glass this day ere the set of sun.' My blood ran cold and even as he said it, I felt a cold chill spreading from the tips of my big toes. Clarissa, who had become greatly agitated, tugged at my hand and both of us, with terror at our hearts, ran through the gathering dusk toward the palace. The sun was sinking fast and before I had gone many paces, I could feel my feet becoming intensely cold. Faster I ran, and with more ardor did Clarissa hurry me on. Gradually my ankles became as cold as ice. I could not bend them as I walked and could not move my toes. Our flight home became slower and slower as I found it more and more difficult to crawl along, until I could go no farther. Sinking down on the grass by the last rays of the setting sun, I beheld the fairy's dreadful curse come true. As the sun sank beneath the hills it lingered for a moment reflected in the transparent solidity of my two poor little glassy feet.

"I could not walk a step, so Clarissa, although loath to leave me, ran on with distressing whimpers to fetch help. As she disappeared into the night, my heart sank. All around me birds who were settling down to sleep peeped out at me; the doves cooing to each other sounded like a melancholy dirge to my unhappy ears. Even the deer crept close to me and with sad soft eyes pityingly beheld my plight. At last, after what seemed hours, I heard voices and could see lanterns coming swinging toward me through the trees.

"Clarissa had roused the whole court, and in a perturbed and frightened multitude they twisted in and out of the tree trunks looking for me. At last Clarissa stood beside me again, once more holding my hand and pressing it to her hairy cheek. While all around me stood the court in dumfounded amazement. 'Alas,' wailed my mother, the Queen, 'She will never be able to dance the minuet at the court ball.' 'Alas,' roared my father, the King, 'she will never be able to kick her ministers of state downstairs.' 'Alas,' sobbed my brother, the heir to the throne, as he bathed my glass feet with hot tears, 'She will never be able to run to meet her sweetheart.'

53

"When they had all spoken, such a babble of voices ensued that it was all I could do to make my story heard. Finally, my story told and incredulously listened to, a litter was called for, into which I was placed, and with the faithful Clarissa sitting by the pillow caressing my golden hair, I was carried in procession back to the palace.

"The news had soon spread there, and it was ablaze with light. Servants ran hither and thither not knowing what to do; the grooms and stable boys crowded the terrace and were with difficulty dispersed by the court chamberlain, so eager were they to see this strange new phenomenon of their Princess with the feet of glass. The peacocks, awakened out of their first slumber by the unusual noise, shrieked with anger; the elephants in my father's hunting stable trumpeted and stamped; the cocks crowed and the dogs bayed, as if they all knew of this strange calamity and were proclaiming the news in chorus to the sparkling heavens. A fiery-tailed comet tore the sky in two, and a distant peal of thunder stirred the sleeping countrymen as if warning them of terrible things to come.

"At last I was carried to my own apartments and was there kindly tended by my brother and my own attendants. My mother and father went to consult the court necromancer to ask him why such a calamity had descended on them, what it meant, and what could be done to bring the life blood back to my feet.

"They were the daintiest, prettiest feet you ever saw. Clad in glass slippers as clear as crystal, they reflected the candle flames and the firelight. They were so elegant to behold that had they but been those of a doll they would have filled me with delight. I was of course unable to walk a step and was therefore dependent on the kind attentions of Clarissa, who was inconsolable. She did all she could to amuse me, playing so prettily with my canary birds, who lived free and fluttering about my room, not caged as Mr. Quizzit cages you, my friends. They perched in the hangings of my bed and sang to me as never before, as if their little hearts would break. They even perched on my feet and admired their own reflections, gently pecking with their beaks at the cold images that pecked back at them.

"The next day, after a troubled night, I was attended by the King and Queen, the court chamberlain, the ministers of state, and the court necromancer, who had come to pronounce what should, in his opinion, be done. They surrounded me in a ring of solemnity, as each one considered the picture of a royal Princess with feet of the finest glass. After some minutes, the necromancer adjusted his spectacles, and taking out a tuning fork and a quizzing glass, he carefully examined my feet from glass heel to glass toe and back again. 'Remove her shoes,' he said. This my brother and Clarissa each did tenderly with infinite care. With the utmost caution he tapped each foot in turn with his tuning fork, setting the end of it against the post of my bed, and listened attentively to the note it gave. It was so bright and clear that it set all my canaries, who had been hushed, so awe-inspired were they by the sight of the entire court, into a frenzy of twittering.

" 'Put on a pair of her slippers,' said he, silencing the birds with the severity of his tone. Gently my brother placed on my feet a pair of the finest red damask dancing slippers decorated with diamond buckles and silver heels. But such a feeling of intense cold had started in my limbs when they first removed my glass slippers, which increased the longer they were off and reached agony when my damask slippers were on my feet, that I was forced to cry out, and had to implore them to put back my glass footwear. Whereupon the circulation was once more restored in my limbs and I felt no more pain. The necromancer looked puzzled but would admit nothing, and so, recommending in a solemn voice that my feet, with slippers complete, should be bathed in a mixture of warm lavender oil and rose water night and morning, he led the way out of the room, attended by the whole court, seriously shaking their heads.

"My brother and Clarissa were most careful to carry out his instructions, and each night and morning for a week they bathed and dried my feet with the utmost care.

"From the evening when this sad bewitchment had fallen upon me, everything seemed to go wrong, large and small, both in the palace and outside it in the wider sphere of my father's realm.

"The palace cook burned the crepe suzette to a frizzle next day at dinner, so that it was uneatable; one of my father's best hunting elephants escaped from its stable and ran trumpeting into the forest, dragging behind it the chains that had secured its great legs; the court hairdresser oversinged the King's beard; my mother's favorite lapdog died; the court fool slipped downstairs and broke his leg; the hens refused to lay; it rained when it should have been fine and was fine when the farmers wanted rain; my father's ambassadors returned from a nearby province and announced that a once-friendly monarchy was about to declare war on us; half the treasure fleet of the kingdom was lost in a terrible storm at sea; news of a forest fire and an attack of the plague was brought in by exhausted messengers from the four corners of the country. Disasters were never-ending.

"In fact, so great and so many were the calamities that seemed to have befallen my country since my affliction that I began to think they were in some way connected. It was not long before the whole court thought the same thing, and dark looks met me wherever I was carried, while unpleasant whispers hissed from mouth to ear as I passed down the corridors. Last but not least to my mind, the faithful Clarissa showed signs of pining away with a broken heart.

"The cure prescribed by the necromancer was of no avail and so my brother, although grieved to leave me in so unfriendly an atmosphere, decided to go off in search of a wise man whose magic was stronger than that of the fairy who had bewitched me.

"He set out alone on his strawberry steed and searched the country high and low. For weeks there arrived at the palace wise men and women by the score, who, dazzled by the sound of the reward that my brother had offered them, made the difficult journey to the palace in order to see and perhaps unglaze my feet. Many and varied were the cures they tried. Some would have my feet thrust into the fire; some gave me unpleasant drinks; some wove a cloud of the deepest spells so that my feet were hardly visible; others just stared and muttered unfathomable words. But no one could dissolve the fixed and solid glassiness of my twin beslippered feet.

"Day after day, week after week, went by. Calamity followed on calamity, until my mother and father were frantic. They were becoming so unpopular with their people for being the parents of this unnatural child who was thought to have brought this chapter of woe on them that they were in despair. More and more infrequent became the visits of my brother's wizards, witches, and wise women, until at last we had news of his return.

"One frosty winter night he galloped into the palace yard, carrying behind him a thin, wizened little bit of a woman, all muffled up in furs and wearing a great high crowned hat of sealskin ornamented with a golden cabalistic sign. This was the last wise woman left in the country and she was said to possess the most extraordinary powers.

"She was hastily brought to my chamber and amidst my brother's expressions of joy at seeing me again, she performed the most careful examination of my feet. Clarissa was greatly weakened and while at all times showed the gentlest of natures, could not be persuaded to show any signs of friendliness to this old dame, and bared her teeth in an angry snarl every time she approached. Her inspection complete, the old woman announced that she thought she could be of use, but was not sure. She said her cure might be effective, but on the other hand it might not. But if my parents wished her to try it, they must promise to carry out her directions to the letter, or even worse calamities would beset the nation for which she would not be answerable. Willingly—too willingly, as you will see—they agreed and implored her to begin.

"Producing two colored powders, she tossed them into the air, producing a flash of fire and a sweet sickly smell. 'A nick rit a nack rit, a boat rik and a bat rik,' the old crone intoned. Whereupon a strange glow was seen to infuse my feet and I felt vague throbbings as if their circulation was returning, but it waned and there lay my feet still as clear as crystal. Three times she repeated her words and threw her powders into the air, and three times a pink flush diffused my feet. But each time it grew weaker until the old woman stopped her magic, and crying out in a weird uncanny voice she screeched, 'Take her out into the depths of the forest and abandon her; then and only then will peace and prosperity be restored to your kingdom. I can do nothing with her feet. Nothing can be done.' Consternation filled the listening court. My brother and Clarissa fell on my neck and bathed me with tears. My father consulted with his ministers and my mother fainted dead away.

"At length they decided they must carry out the old woman's demands, and so amidst much wailing and lamentation my litter was taken out through the snow-covered park into the forest. By force my heartbroken brother was torn from me, and with scalding tears we parted from each other. Clarissa, who was too weak to stand, had refused to be dragged from me. Together we were left in a hollow in the snow. As the lights of the court attendants drew away from us and the cries of my brother grew fainter, a great heaviness descended on me and it began once more to snow.

"The soft flakes fell silently down through the trees, glistening like diamonds in the starlight, gently caressing the icy brilliance of my feet. Clarissa's hand in mine was warm, but it was the only warmth about me, for as the snow covered us both, my whole body began to freeze from my feet upwards, and their crystal transparency began to spread. My legs, my knees, my thighs, were gradually turning to glass. Clarissa, mute with misery and weakness, could do nothing but kiss my fast-glazing fingers. 'Take one of my rings, dear Clarissa, for I shall soon be all glass; one day my brother will find you and by this alone he will know you.' As I said these words, the strange lack of feeling that accompanied the progress of the glass reached my wrists and throat and I could say no more. With the last power of sight from my fast-glazing eyeballs, I saw Clarissa carefully removing the ring from my glassy finger. As the life ebbed from it, it seemed to flow into Clarissa, for she appeared to revive, and with all the pent-up emotion of a loving friend she beat her breast and kept her warm hand on my chilling brow. As the crown of my head became glass, Clarissa let forth a low cry. As the glass had grown upon me, my life spirit had entered into the almost dead form of Clarissa, and as the last hair of my head became a strand of glass I realized that I was now looking through Clarissa's eyes at the clear crystal form of a beautiful Princess that, until a moment ago, had been myself.

"Imagine my astonishment! I was able to run once more, if

only in the guise of a poor dumb ape. So leaving the snow-covered statue of my former self, I set out in search of warmth and deliverance. On and on I traveled through the snow, hopelessly lost in the dense forest. The owls hooted and the wolves howled, but I was not frightened for now I was a wild beast like themselves. The deer looked at me with their mild eyes as I loped past, but did not run from me. The fox and the badger stopped in their midnight prowl to give me a greeting, and the rabbits sheltering in their burrows looked out at me with smiles of friendliness.

"Suddenly the snow gave way before me, and I found myself snug and warm at the bottom of a deep hole lined with leaves and bracken. As I could neither climb out nor see any way of escape, I nestled down among the leaves and fell asleep. I awoke in the morning to find our Mr. Quizzit looking down on me. He was out catching wild beasts and birds to stock his animal shop, and I had unwittingly fallen into one of his traps. How I was brought to England is another and longer story, but here I am, the royal inhabitor of my faithful Clarissa's mortal form, wearing my ring so that one day my brother will recognize me, and with the love and goodness that is in his heart will be able to free me from my double enchantment."

By this time all the animals in the shop were so saddened by this pathetic story that nothing could be heard by Theodosia and Verney as they crept to bed but the open sobbing of the armadillo and the sniveling of some of the smaller birds.

At length the dodo, clearing his throat and thanking the ape politely, said that for his part he voted that their next storyteller should be sure and tell them a gay tale, or they would all die of broken hearts and never live to hear his story, which he vowed would set them all into such a twitter of excitement it was well worth waiting for.

It was therefore decided that the next night the caterpillars should tell their story, as they claimed it was to be a story full of promise, neither depressing nor sad.

The next day when Theodosia and Verney were in the shop they asked the ape-princess to show them her ring; with silent docile gestures of despair the poor beast brushed aside the long hair that concealed it and showed them the carved gold ring set with its great green stone that seemed to hold the greenness of the mossiest forest pool and the bright fires of the aurora borealis. With astonishment they blew out their lips and whistled with admiration, so magnificent and valuable did it look.

## Chapter V

# NIGHT THE FOURTH . . . THURSDAY
# . . . THE CATERPILLARS' TALE

*C*LIP, clip, clip, clip, munch, munch, munch," began the caterpillars, as they took a few hasty bites from some fresh leaves
before opening their mandibles to speak. Letting go of the twigs
with their hard front true legs, and clinging to the bark with
their fleshy false legs, they swayed their helmeted heads from
side to side in unison like a chain of snakes under the spell of a
snake charmer. "We," they sang in chorus, "have already known
two situations in life and are shortly to know two more. We are
therefore to be envied if it is your desire to live a life of variety,
but pitied if you wish to lead the sedentary life of a recluse.
We were once eggs." Here half their company ceased singing
and began to clip, clip, clip, munch at the leaves again, while
the others proceeded with their story.

"We were once eggs, laid on the delicate leaves of a piece of
hog's fennel; our plant grew in some swampy ground in the
middle of a very deep forest. Its flat creamy heads of flowers

gently moved in the shade of willow trees like saucers of milk, spilling their acrid fragrance on the breeze. One day a centaur maiden searching for violets and long-stalked kingcups to twine garlands for her brow smelled our flowers' scent mingled with trodden watercress and honeysuckle. Plucking the whole plant, she wove it into a tiara with briar roses and white bryony, yellow mimulus and blue forget-me-nots. With flat cool lily leaves from a nearby pool, she crowned her golden tresses, and placing the wreath on them, she ran thus garlanded to meet her centaur lover. A centaur, you must know, is a creature whose human head and body sprouts from the shoulders of a horse, so that it is endowed with the sagacity and deft fingers of a human together with the speed and vigor of four strong hooves. They are said to be the descendants of the offspring of Centaurus, son of Apollo and Stilbia.

"The glades of this forest were inhabited by beings seldom seen by man: nymphs and dryads gamboled about the woodland pools chasing each other through the trees. Satyrs peered with curving horns and shaggy flanks, stamping their cloven feet at hamadryads in the trees. Unicorns cropped the grass and dashed headlong through the bushes when danger threatened. Once a century a phoenix burst into flame on the topmost tree, flying with weird cries amid showers of sparks into the upper air. The trees flowered more luxuriantly than anywhere else; winter hardly seemed to penetrate the center of the forest, so dense was the undergrowth and so thickly grew the trees. Harpies, in whose ugly bodies are said to dwell the tormented souls of those who have died by their own hand, inhabited the outskirts of this forest, which perhaps accounted for the fact that it was unfrequented by but a few mortals. Lost travelers stumbled into it at nightfall, only to leave it as soon as it was day; intrepid gypsies visited it to collect the rare herbs that grew there from which to concoct the magic potions that only gypsies know. But by the people of that part of the country it was suspiciously shunned."

Here the second band of caterpillars, who had been busily eating throughout their brethren's story, ceased munching and rose to take up the thread of the story where the first speakers had left off. They in their turn bent down and commenced eating exactly where the others had finished.

"From our elevated station on the centaur's garlanded brow, we were hatched from our eggs in the warm sunlight; as fresh new caterpillars we surveyed the landscape and were quick to descry our centaur's lover stamping impatiently, his broad brown body flashing proudly in the sun. Embracing lovingly, they pranced off across the greensward, their arms affectionately joined, their bodies linked by a chain of cowslips and eglantine.

"She was a milk-white steed, if you can call a centaur such, with light creamy skin and the complexion of the softest rose, golden-haired and blue-eyed. The radiancy of her light eyes reflected the dark pools of his, which were a deep and smoldering violet. His flanks were blotched all over with irregular marks of black and white like sunlit islands, his nut-brown human skin shone alike with his horse's mane.

"All that day we rode on the unclouded brow of the centaur

through glade and forest, until toward evening, when the exhausted lovers lay down on a bank, she took our garland with a languid hand and tossed it into a nut bush, beneath which they were lying.

"Once more at rest but now on a fast-wilting and uneatable plant, off we all went in search of a new plant of hog's fennel. Soon we found one growing near a stream, so with one accord we claimed it as our own and ascended to the top to start eating downwards toward the bottom leaves of the plant. We stayed there for several days hardly aware of what went on around us so hungry had we become. It seemed to us that the most important thing in the world for us to do was to stuff and stuff and stuff with food, until we felt our skins nearly bursting. At last we were overcome by a terrible feeling of repletion and a desire to get away from our fellow caterpillars to the peace of a leaf each one by himself.

"One by one we retired to the underside of a leaf, where to our mutual surprise, our skins, having become so incredibly tight, did actually burst, and splitting down the middle, we stepped out of our old worn-out skins arrayed in gleaming new ones, complete with a new appetite in the bargain. Away we went to our dinners with more of a will than ever until one day, when not paying enough attention to what was going on about us, so busy with our eating were we, to our surprise we found ourselves swept into a little dry box by the hand of a collector named Moses Harris, who after studying us for some time, sold us to Mr. Quizzit a few days ago.

"Now, if you will excuse us," they said, "we must return to our brethren and complete our feasting as we are once more overcome with an overpowering wish to eat. In fact we are famished," they mumbled between mouthfuls of food, for they seemed too hungry to wait any longer. All that could be heard was a steady clip, clip, munch, munch as before.

As it was still dark and there were quite a few more hours to go until dawn, the animals were at first puzzled what to do. But they didn't remain so long, for they suddenly heard a muffled, wrapped-up sort of voice saying, "I will carry the story of my brethren the caterpillars one stage further." It came from inside the caterpillars' muslin tent, though exactly where it was difficult to say, but one of the parrots observed a fat chrysalis give a wriggle at the same time as the voice was heard, so it was passed around from cage to cage that one of the chrysalides was now the speaker.

"My brethren are so hungry for they are shortly going to enter the third stage of their life history," said the chrysalis. "That is to say, they are about to pupate, and naturally they will need to fill themselves up with a good store of food. I myself pupated soon after we got here as I came of an earlier brood than they did, but their time is just nigh. They will eat until they can eat no longer and their skins feel like splitting, when once more they will be overcome by a desire for solitude and will each walk away into a corner. Here they will carefully spin a little pad of silk on the twig they have chosen. They will let themselves down from it until they are hanging by their twin

69

claspers. Then with a sharp crack their skins will split from head to tail and, with a convulsive wriggle, they will emerge as a shining new chrysalis, not another caterpillar as one might expect, for this is the next stage through which they have to pass. Inside this jeweled casket with the lacquer exterior that I too am proud to wear, there is enacted one of the most profound mysteries of nature."

All this time the voice had been extremely indistinct and muffled, as if it were speaking like a soldier whose head was wound around with several layers of bandage. The animals had to crane their necks and listen very hard.

"Inside the darkness of this close prison, I am changing myself from being an ugly, ungainly, green and black caterpillar, able to go only on four legs and a pair of claspers, waving the rest of my legs and body in a blind groping way before me. From this, I say, I am changing myself into one of the most beautiful flies in nature, able to soar into the bright heavens from daybreak until sunset. I shall be a delicate, creamy, sulphur yellow, with an intricate tracery of black on my glossy wings and a spot of red and blue near the two tails that give to my graceful wings the name that I shall bear—'Swallowtail.'

"It is wonderfully dark in here, airless and prodigious cold. I scarcely know myself which is my head and which my feet, so closely packed am I. I feel as if I am about to explode, I'm so cramped and stifled. But I know my time is not yet ripe.

"Tell me, as I can tell you no more about myself and have had no experiences to tell you of, what this world into which I am about to burst is like. I feel so confident that it must be full of promise and so very beautiful. Tell me each in turn what I am to expect, I pray you."

"It is a strange world you are coming to," said the parrot, "full of many sorts of men both good and evil."

"It is a wide world you are coming to," said the bear, "full of men who will betray each other for a few silver coins."

"It is a topsy-turvy world you are coming to, where men, who are among the weaker animals, rule over the strong and mighty beasts by reason of their brains and their ability to think," said the snake, surprising all of them by his utterance as he had never spoken before.

"It is a world full of all kinds of good food, if you can get it," greedily cried the fish.

"Yes, it is indeed," chorused the mice hastily, when they heard something that they could heartily agree with, as they hadn't the wit to think of anything original themselves.

"It is a dark world," wailed the bats.

"It is a wide world," cawed the rooks.

"It is a superstitious world," smiled the salamander.

"It is a world full of sorrow," sobbed the ape.

"It is a world to be fought," crowed the gamecock.

"Or tricked," slyly whispered the raccoon.

"It is a weary world," yawned the armadillo, turning over in his sleep.

"It appears to be a world full of contradictions," sighed the chrysalis. "For none of you agree with each other. Anyhow, it seems to be full of opportunities if one has a mind to prosper in it. I believe I shall soon be entering it for I feel more constricted than ever, and I don't think my jerkin can possibly stand it much longer."

"Your color is changing," said one of the caterpillars to the chrysalis, as he looked up from his incessant feeding. "You are getting much darker and all the sparkle is going out of you." "It is very unusual," said a large Camberwell Beauty who was resting on a twig nearby in her plum-colored crinoline edged with yellow lace. "For I have never heard of a chrysalis hatching out in the middle of the night, but I daresay it has been caused by all this talking you have been going in for." "Anything might happen now, I shouldn't wonder," growled a White Admiral testily.

"I am hatching, I am hatching," sang out the voice of the chrysalis, much louder and clearer than before; and with a tearing noise its prickly outer jacket tore, and out swung a shapeless wet bundle like a damp, crumpled cambric handkerchief. Gently it swung on the now colorless chrysalis shell. On closer inspection, the animals who were near enough to see through the muslin curtain could see that the shapeless bundle had legs and two slender clubbed antennae and that gradually it was revolving, opening out, taking on a definite shape. By degrees the wings, which they now recognized those creased black and yellow bags to be, were being inflated; with convulsive wobbles the newly hatched fly shook itself. As yet it was all long striped body and head with slim legs, which it moved carefully as if testing their strength. Gradually the wings filled out until, there before their wondering eyes, at the top of the twig, towards which it had been climbing as its wings grew, there perched a perfect swallowtail butterfly.

"O joy! I am out at last and can move my antennae, flap my wings, and dance with my feet," cried the swallowtail as she pirouetted on her twig. "O for the sunshine and freedom so that I can court the beautiful flowers that bloom especially for our delight."

"Poor thing, she is going to be sadly disillusioned," wailed the ever-pessimistic ape.

"No, no, do not disappoint her," gruffly growled the bear, "for I know that when Arabella comes down tomorrow and sees the beauty of our swallowtail's bright new wings she will set her free at once."

"Maybe, maybe," said the ape.

"Of course she will, she must, she must," cried all the animals together. In such earnestness as if the question of their own freedom was at stake. For they all felt deep concern for the new butterfly, for hadn't they all seen her born and almost taken part in half her life history? Here the children crouched on the stairs resolved to free the frail butterfly beauty as soon as possible.

"I feel you coming, sunny dawn," cried the butterfly. "Do not tarry. O rose, O lily, I shall be with you ere long, and know the secrets of your hearts for you will not be able to hide them from my long searching tongue," she gaily threatened.

"Give our love to the sky," sang the linnets.

73

"And ours to the sun," trilled the larks.

"And ours to the moon," whispered the bats.

"Ours to the rippling waters," bubbled the fish.

"And ours to all the flowers of the wood and meadow," cooed the doves as the first rays of the rising sun filtered through the shutters, and the animals heard the clank of the pump handle as Silas sluiced his tousled head under the pump in the back yard.

As Silas began removing the shutters, the dodo just had time to nod his thanks to the butterfly and her attendant caterpillars who still went on eating. In a muffled croak he called on one of the fish to think up a story to regale them with that evening just as Silas stumped into the shop still rubbing the sleep out of his eyes.

Another night of midnight listening rendered the little Quizzits into frail, wide-eyed ghosts with white cheeks and dark rings under their eyes. As they yawned their way through breakfast, Arabella, so as not to alarm them, drew her husband's attention silently to their children and pointed significantly to the big brown bottle of jalap that stood on the dresser with a large spoon balanced across its broad cork. Mr. Quizzit nodded, and when Theodosia and Verney asked to be allowed to get down he looked over his spectacles and said that they could, but they were to bring the bottle to him. Reluctantly they did so and stood dutifully before him, their eyes tight shut, their hands behind their backs, and their tummies stuck out.

"Open your mouths," said their father kindly but firmly.

"You both look pale, we'll see if a spoonful of this won't bring back the roses to your cheeks." Their mother wiped away a tear from her eye with the corner of her apron so touched was she by the quiet way they took the medicine that they hated. Smiles however soon returned all around the breakfast table when they were each given a spoonful of quince jelly to take away the nasty taste and for being such good uncomplaining children.

Little did their parents suspect them, or the animals, of their nightly pranks.

## Chapter VI

## NIGHT THE FIFTH . . . FRIDAY
## . . . THE GOLDEN CARP'S TALE

*O*N the fifth night of the animals' nightly entertainment, when
Theodosia and Verney were preparing to come down and listen
for the third time, their father was awakened by an unusual
noise. Something in the street had woken him, a late sedan chair
or an unusually loud-voiced night watchman; he lay thinking
about his children, his wife, and his shop full of animals. As is
the wont of problems at such an hour of the night, they weighed
more overpoweringly on him than ever they did during the
daytime. He lay for a long time tossing and turning until at last
he woke Arabella also.

Sitting up in bed in their white nightcaps, they fell to discussing the mutual problems of their uncomplicated life, accompanied by a gentle murmur from the shop beneath. When they
had discussed everything they could think of they became silent.
As they sat there Mr. Quizzit was suddenly struck by the lack of

noise coming from the shop below, accustomed as he was to the usual hubbub. But the quiet bubbling voice of the carp, who had just begun his tale, was all that he could hear.

Silently Mr. and Mrs. Quizzit stole out of bed and tiptoed to the top of the stairs. Here on the landing, hidden from their children by the turn in the staircase, they could hear quite clearly the silver, bell-like tones of the carp's tale.

Being Friday night and near the end of the week, all the animals were tired and jaded. "I don't know," began the oval voice of the fish bubbling up from the green depths of his aquarium, "whether I can tell a whole long story for I haven't the sort of brain that can think of one thing for very long at a time, except food. But I will try. It may be in short incidents, rather disjointed, like ants' eggs scattered on the water, and not a long string like frogs' spawn, but I will endeavor to entertain you." Here everyone perked up a bit, for it sounded promising.

"The land I come from is on the other side of the world. Everything is indeed very different from here. It is separated from its neighboring state by a long fortified wall that winds over mountain and valley many hundreds of miles; it is so broad that a coach and four may be driven along it with ease. On the other three sides it is protected by a range of lofty mountains, a desert, and the ocean.

"The inhabitants of this country are small and dainty in stature, their skin varies in color from deep olive to light lemon. They have small dark eyes that appear as slits in their faces, for their skin folds over them in such a way as to give their eyes a delicate almond shape. Some of their curious customs I will relate to you.

"I will start with the top of their heads. The men, who effect a very pompous mien, grow their hair very long at the crown, and drawing it all together, plait it into a long rope or pigtail in which they take great pride. To have this pigtail cut off would be to them a great disgrace. The women, who behave with great modesty, wear their hair braided into two large lobes or knots, having the appearance of a cottage loaf, which they adorn with flowers and ornaments of gold and silver. Both men and women wear long silken gowns with very wide sleeves, embroidered with the most beautiful patterns of flowers and birds. The men wear padded coats and little hard pillbox hats, while the women swath their outer garments with a broad girdle several feet in width which they arrange in a formal bow behind. The workmen in the fields in wet weather wear broad-brimmed hats and cloaks made of plaited straw.

"At an early age the poor unfortunate female infants have their tiny feet cruelly warped by tight bandages, which so deform them that their growth is retarded. For the rest of their lives they patter about in very high clogs, as grown women on little feet like dolls, carrying folded paper fans and paper parasols to keep off the angry rays of the sun, which together with the rest of their modest delicacy gives them an appearance of unreal waxworks.

"They use neither knife nor fork nor spoon, for all their food comes to the table already cut small. Together with a vast

79

quantity of rice, they devour it from small china bowls with two wooden or ivory implements like straight sticks, called chopsticks. These they use most deftly, never once spilling their food, notwithstanding they eat at a great rate. They consume a great deal of weak green tea with their food. This, like the rice, which as I say they eat in abundance, is grown on the terraced slopes of their hills.

"The young boys, and even old men, take great delight in flying kites. These are designed in all sorts of quaint shapes and to an enormous size. I have seen one the exact replica of myself but the size of a porpoise. Dragons, of which there appear a great number in all their artistic creations, and birds figure a great deal on their kites.

"I cannot remember a great deal more to tell you of their habits, but will consider," the fish suddenly announced just when everyone was getting interested. So saying, he sank to the bottom of his tank where he nibbled at some food, but soon rose again and went on.

"Ah! yes, their methods of catching both fresh- and saltwater fish are most singular," he went on, shuddering. "In the spawning season, countrymen go into the upper reaches of many rivers where the fish are known to gather, and fill great earthenware jars full of spawn that they sell to the merchants, who in turn sell them to rich men and nobles who turn them into their fish ponds, thus restocking them with a swarm of new fish when they, in due season, hatch out. It was in this fashion that I myself was taken.

"I lived in the fish pond of a very venerable white-bearded merchant. It was well stocked with goldfish, rainbow trout, angelfish, carp, and many other friends and relations of mine, both large and small. We were fed twice a day with cooked rice and dried insects, a variety of food chosen to appeal to all appetites.

"Besides the merchant's five beautiful daughters, he had once been the proud father of a beautiful youth. This is how his adoring family lost him.

"This youth was as radiant as the sun but he was in love with the daughter of a demon. She was as beautiful as the moon, for her evil father had made her so in order to ensnare a poor foolish mortal. When she looked into our pool at night, her reflection looked up at her wedded to that of the moon like the portait of two twin sisters. Despite the evil of her father, she was a good girl and had fallen in love with the boy Tachibana against her own and her father's will. They met each night, facing one another across the waters of our pool, always divided by its glistening waters.

"The merchant's property adjoined that of the demon, but they were divided by a thick growth of bamboo and a high wall, in the middle of which was our pool, forming an opening but at the same time a barrier between the two estates. Tachibana would come at sundown to his side and Kikujido to hers at the rising of the moon. Many were the soft sorrowful sighs we heard them cast like pebbles in our pool; many were the kisses they blew like ripples on the surface of the water.

"The demon's intention was to entice Tachibana across the pool toward his daughter but to drown him on the way, for he was jealous of his beauty and wished to destroy him; but his daughter, because of the love she bore the boy, prevented him from crossing with a different excuse each night. One night it was, 'Oh, do not cross, dear Tachibana, for I hear my father approaching'; the second, 'Oh, do not cross, I beg of you, Tachibana, for I see your father coming through the trees.' The third, 'Oh, do not cross, Tachibana, for it is too dark.' The fourth, 'Oh, do not cross, I pray thee, dear Tachibana, or you will catch your death of cold.' The fifth, 'Oh, do not, I beseech you, cross, Tachibana, for a poisonous fish may bite you.' The sixth, 'Oh, do not cross for the moon is bright and one of your sisters is I am certain watching us.' And so she went on, at her wits' end to think of a new excuse each night.

"At length Tachibana could wait no longer to embrace his beloved, and casting off his sandals he began to wade into the water. 'Tachibana, Tachibana, I pray and beseech you, go back, go back, I beg of you,' cried Kikujido in great distress, 'I implore you go back,' but he came on. She could stand it no longer, and daring her father's anger, she blurted out, 'Go back, my beloved Tachibana, go back, for my father is a wicked demon and he intends to drown you ere you reach the other side. Stay where you are and we can at least meet each night and mingle our sighs together, but come a step closer to me and you will surely perish and I shall die of grief.'

"Whereupon her father the demon, who had been concealed

all this time among the bamboo bushes, rushed forth and in a great rage transformed them both into apricot trees, condemning them to stand facing each other across the water for the rest of eternity. But there they outwitted him, for they soon grew and grew until their branches intertwined over our depths. Each year their branches became more and more interlaced until you could scarcely distinguish between them. The most beautiful sight in the whole country was in springtime to see these two loving trees ablaze with blossom mirrored in our moonlit waters.

"The neighboring demons and their wives were so appalled by such heartless cruelty that they called a meeting to decide how they could best compensate the merchant for the loss of his son, for they were unable to break the demon's spell. They declared that they would endow each of his daughters with the most singular gift. The first found herself able at will to blow with the breath from her mouth any animal she wished to name; the second in the same way could produce any food she wished; the third, any precious stone; the fourth, any flower; and the fifth and youngest, any form of music they cared to listen to.

"As you will soon see, these were wonderful gifts to possess, and the old merchant was able to retire and lead a happy life amidst great luxury. The only care he possessed since the loss of his son was that he had terrible nightmares. But this was soon put to rights; for the eldest daughter summoned up a Baku with a deep breath. Each night, stationed at the head of the old man's bed, he devoured the bad dreams as fast as they formed, and breathed out good ones for the sleeper to enjoy.

"Each day at mealtimes they all sat on the floor in a circle cross-legged—for they do not have tables in this country—holding their chopsticks in one hand and their bowls in the other. When their father had said a few words of thanks and praise to his ancestors, his second daughter said, 'Very well, now what would you all like?'

"One said she would like crispy noodles with lobster; another, curried chicken; the next, fried vegetables and bamboo shoots; the youngest said she would like nothing better than a bowl of kumquat oranges in syrup; while their father said he would have sharksfin soup and boiled rice that they could all share; and his second daughter said she would have pancake rolls all to herself. So one, two, three, puff, four, five, six, puff—there lay the food all steaming hot and of the best quality before them, ready to be eaten. When they had eaten their fill, there was still a lot left. 'What a shame,' said the father, 'to waste all this good food.' 'We will soon see to that,' said his eldest daughter, who sighing deeply brought forth a whole troupe of little Pekingese dogs who soon demolished the food that was left.

"When they had rested and slept a little after their excellent repast, they all retired from the house into the garden, and beneath the shade of his bewitched son, the merchant and his five daughters sat enjoying their leisure. The youngest blew out her cheeks now and again and their ears were assailed by the sweetest music in the world. The third daughter with a few elegant sighs filled her lap with the most beautiful pearls, which she and her sisters set themselves to threading into necklets and ropes to adorn themselves. The fourth daughter breathed a wreath of lotus blossoms for each of her sisters, a bunch of pink-scented peonies for her father, and all were contented.

"As can be imagined, they could not keep these strange gifts to themselves, for if the youngest daughter went out into company, everyone was very puzzled when they suddenly were surrounded by the sweet sounds of music when no musicians were present. Soon it got about that the old merchant and his daughters had been so favored by the demons that people were all the time asking advice, hoping for gifts of jewels and precious stones. But the merchant was very shrewd and he commanded his daughters to be careful how they used their gifts when away from home, for if they used them imprudently they might very well regret it, and become not only the envy of everyone but also in danger of the wiles of wicked characters.

"They but seldom went out therefore beyond the gates of their father's estate, and then always two sisters together. If they went to stay with any of their relations, the eldest blew out her cheeks hard and produced two horses on which two of the girls seated themselves. The fourth sister gave breath to a sheaf of lilies to give their relatives as a present. If it was to humble relatives that they were going, the second sister would always go so that she could produce a rare banquet for them; but if it was to proud relatives, then the third sister would go and give each of her relations, down to the smallest baby, presents of such magnificent stones—amethysts, rubies, emeralds, and diamonds of such brilliance and luster—that the pride of even the most exalted was very soon brought down.

"I must add that I knew of these happenings because the

sisters would discuss with their father all that they had done or intended to do, at the foot of their apricot brother by the side of our fish pool."

Here the carp stopped and slowly descended to the bottom of the aquarium, where he was again seen to nibble quickly at something; then with a train of bubbles, he rose once more to the surface and picked up the thread of his narrative. "I beg your pardon," he said, "but I felt a bit peckish. I will go on if you are so disposed." Cries of "Yes, yes, do, by all means" greeted him on every hand, so after several silent mouthings and gapes from side to side, he started off.

"One day, when the demon had been dead a long time, exactly ten years after he had transformed the lovers, as this happy family were seated by their apricot tree they were suddenly puzzled by a violent trembling and agitation in all its branches. At last the eldest sister said, 'Pray what is it, brother, do you wish to tell us something?' Whereupon the tree bent its branches as if it were nodding and then stopped as abruptly as it had begun. The sisters crowded around the tree's rough black trunk, and pressing each an ear to it, they called out gently, 'Speak to us, speak to us, Tachibana, what is it you have to say?' Straining their ears until they thought their heads would burst, they at last heard a very tiny, small, thin voice, the voice of their brother, which seemed to come from very deep down in the ground. It said, 'I have learned from the spirit of a good demon who dwells snugly at my roots that there is a way to save Kikujido and myself from further confinement in the forms of these two trees. It is this. My eldest sister must go to the source of the mighty river Yangtse, where she will find a magic apricot stone. If she returns with this we shall once more resume our mortal shape.' Having said this, the voice died away and the tree again became as still as it had ever been.

" 'Alas and alack,' cried all the sisters, 'how will you ever get there, and once there how will you find the stone?' They were in a high state of flutter, for they knew not what course was best to take, nor could the old merchant advise them for he was so excited at the thought of the return of his beloved son.

"However, we carp at the bottom of the pool knew the secret, as we too were friendly with the good demon's spirit; after a hasty discussion among us, it was decided that as I was the strongest in the pool, I should offer to carry Tachibana's eldest sister on my back. We therefore all rose to the surface and, in a ring, with me in the center, we made our proposition to the wondering girl. 'Why gladly,' she answered, 'will I ride on your back. But how shall we reach the banks of the Yangtse?' 'That is easy,' said I. 'Fetch me a crystal bowl to ride in, breathe us the swiftest horse you can find in your lungs, and we shall get there in no time.' Without more ado, a bowl was fetched and filled with water, and into it I hopped. Her sister of the jeweled breath sighed forth a dazzling array of precious stones that my passenger wore, in case of emergencies, and so seated on her horse with my bowl fixed before her on the crupper, we sped off across rice fields and tea gardens toward the yellow waters of the Yangtse.

"At length, at the end of two days' hard galloping, we saw the wide water we were seeking spread out before us, running as far as the eye could see in both directions and crowded with junks and the strangest craft carrying cargoes from port to port.

" 'Here at last' said the sister, 'is the Yangtse. Now our journey really begins.' 'Pour me in, pour me in,' I cried, for I was eager to start. In I went, crying hastily for her to ascend my back; this she did without hesitation, and with her so mounted and gripping firmly to my scales, I began to swim upstream against the current.

"With my heavy burden, it was a hard task to fight against such a swift river and I was hampered by having to dodge in and out of the passing shipping with which the water seethed. At last after a week and a half's traveling, we came to the edge of a great plain where the river had narrowed to a mere thread and hardly trickled along. Across this plain meandered the lazy coils of the stream, until at last now in only a few inches of water we came to the foot of a mountain where sat the goddess DiChu, spooning up the water from a well with her silver ladle thus starting the trickle that later on was to become the mighty Yangtse.

" 'Tell me, O gentle goddess, where I may find the apricot stone that holds the secret of my brother's enchantment, for you are surely the source of the Yangtse.' 'Nay, it is not here,' answered the goddess in a silvery voice. 'You must try the goddess Bukamanga whom you will find at the top of this mountain.' Here she stopped spooning and waved her ladle toward the steeps of the purple mountain at the foot of which she was sitting, whose summit was hidden in the clouds. 'Ah, me,' said the sister, turning to me. 'My journey is not at an end, I must go on farther; but you rest a while here for you will need your strength for our return journey.' So saying, she blew from her mouth a hare, and mounting on its back, she sped off and away up the side of the mountains.

"Up and up they climbed until they were out of sight of the plain beneath. The higher they went the colder it grew. Steeper and rockier became the path, until the hare brought her through the clouds to the feet of the goddess Bukamanga, who sat amidst the rocks before a brazier of charcoal, melting the snow that filled the well of the goddess DiChu at the foot of the mountain.

" 'Tell me, Oh, tell me please, Goddess Bukamanga, where I can find the apricot stone that holds the secret of my brother's enchantment.' 'There is no apricot stone here, little mortal,' said the goddess. 'You must try the goddess Omodaka who dwells in the sky above.' So saying, she waved her arm upwards toward the heavy snow clouds that billowed above. 'Alas,' cried the sister, 'but I will not be daunted now I have come so far.' So telling the exhausted hare to wait, she blew forth a swallow, who, taking her between his wings, soared up aloft and mounted on the cloud.

"Here she found the goddess Omodaka enthroned in white cloud and nursing on her lap her baby. 'Tell me, Oh, tell me, I beg of you, dear Goddess Omodaka, that this is the end of my journey and that you can give me the apricot stone that holds the secret of my brother's enchantment," implored the sister, in fear and trembling before the imposing goddess. 'Hush, mortal,

89

or you will wake my baby and usher up wails like the east wind; but take up his rattle carefully, in it you will find the stone. Wrap it in your leather bag and you may go your way.' With great difficulty the sister opened the rattle, and placing a diamond from her leather bag in its place, she withdrew the stone and wrapped it away carefully. 'It was wise of you to replace it with another stone, for with your diamond he will be able to make lightning to accompany the thunder of his storms,' said the goddess Omodaka.

"Thanking the goddess politely, the sister once more climbed on the back of the swallow and flew down to the top of the mountain. As she left the cloud, the baby woke up, shook his rattle, and cried in a voice like the east wind. A clap of thunder was heard, preceded by the first flash of lightning ever to be seen, which brought on a heavy fall of snow. Once more on the mountain she found the goddess Bukamanga amidst the whirling snowflakes, furiously blowing on her brazier with a little bellows.

"Thanking the goddess for her help, she mounted the hare once more and descended to the plain. Here she found the goddess DiChu in a frenzy of ladling. Thanking her in her turn, and dismissing the swallow and the hare with half the jewels each from her leather bag, she once more mounted the slippery saddle of my scales and we set off for home.

"This time the journey proved easy going and within less than a week we were once more at the point from which we had started. Her horse was quietly cropping the grass, waiting for us beside my crystal bowl, back into which I popped, and away we galloped.

"We reached home to find the four sisters and their father eagerly awaiting us. Carefully Tachibana's sister drew forth her leather bag and took out the stone. As she did so, a breeze seemed to spring up from nowhere and stirred the branches of the two apricot trees until their blossoms fell off in showers into the water. She gave me the stone, and I descended to the botton of the pool; here near the roots of the tree, it had been decided after consultation with the good demon's spirit, the stone must be cracked and the kernel devoured at once to break the enchantment.

"As the sisters and father of Tachibana gathered around their beloved tree, I handed the apricot stone to old Weihaiwei the crayfish, who taking it between two of his strong claws cracked it in two. Pulling out the kernel, we carp descended on it and it was swallowed in a mouthful by the fish nearest to it. At once rising to the surface we beheld a wondrous sight. There beside the water of our pool, in place of the two apricot trees, stood Tachibana and Kikujido, happily beaming on their overjoyed relatives. They stood together with their arms about each other's shoulders and their long hair entwined as the branches of the two trees had been.

"His five sisters each for a moment felt a catch in their breath, then found that with the end of their brother's enchantment they had each lost the gift that the friendly demons had given them. With cries of joy Tachibana's father embraced his beautiful son and radiant new daughter; with tears of gladness Tachibana's sisters smothered them with kisses."

The last few words of the fish's story were drowned by the

water, for before he had properly finished he was impatiently descending to the bottom of the aquarium to finish eating whatever it was he had there, at which he had nibbled during the telling of his story.

"Thank you," said the dodo, "that was very kind. Tomorrow being Saturday and a day for adventure I will call on our friend the bear to favor us with the story of one of his escapades, which I am sure will be very exciting."

When the carp had finished his tale Theodosia and Verney climbed the stairs to bed. They could scarcely believe their eyes, as they rubbed them with sleep, to see their mother and father sitting on the top of the stairs exactly as they had been sitting on the bottom. Nor could their parents, in their turn, believe the evidence of their own eyes when they saw their children coming up the stairs when they thought they had been soundly sleeping above them. Arabella Quizzit had to blow her nose for she had found the story of the apricot-tree lovers pretty but sad, and the sight of her children in the middle of the night in an unexpected place looking so small, white, and vulnerable was altogether too much for her. So that all thought of harsh words to do with them being out of bed were forgotten as she clasped them to her and then tucked them up in bed, where they were instantly asleep without any explanation from either side.

# Chapter VII

# NIGHT THE SIXTH . . . SATURDAY . . . THE BEAR'S TALE

*A*T breakfast on this Saturday all the Quizzit family were very silent, serious, and pale. None of them had slept as much as they were used to and all wondered who was going to do the explaining. Consequently they were silent, then all began talking at once and then as quickly fell silent again. At last Theodosia rose to her feet and in her firm quiet voice began to speak:

"As the eldest I will explain why Verney and I were not in bed and why we look so pale. We do not need any jalap because there is quite another explanation."

Mr. and Mrs. Quizzit looked from one to the other, and Mr. Quizzit moved his spectacles up to his brow as he regarded his daughter respectfully. Arabella's eyes characteristically began to moisten, so poignant did she find the sight of her daughter standing, as it were, in the dock before her parents. But they were not angry, only mystified and a little worried by their children's lack of sleep.

"Last night was the third night we listened to the animals' stories. We do not know why they tell them; the parrot invited us to hear his tale but we couldn't keep awake and so we missed it. The next day he gave us some sunflower seeds to put under the sheet and then it was so uncomfortable we could not sleep."

When she heard this explanation of the presence of the sunflower seeds, Arabella smiled as she remembered how puzzled she and the little maid-of-all-work had been when they made the children's bed.

"The dodo seems to be a kind of chairman," went on Theodosia, "and chooses the storytellers each night. Do please let us hear the story again tonight for the bear is going to speak and the dodo said it was going to be an exciting escapade."

"Knowing the bear and the extent of his travels I shouldn't wonder," said Mr. Quizzit firmly, but seeing how Verney's face fell, he looked across at Arabella and said, "What do you think, Arabella, my love? Shouldn't they have a good night's sleep?"

"Yes, my dear, they should indeed; but how would it be if they went to bed for the afternoon, hibernated as it were, and then it wouldn't matter so much their missing sleep of a night."

"A capital suggestion," agreed Joseph Quizzit at once, who in truth wanted the excuse to hear the story also. "We will all listen together after we have had an afternoon nap."

That night the whole Quizzit family assembled on the stairs warmly wrapped in shawls and sitting on cushions, their eyes goggling with anticipation and excitement.

"Well," said the bear, "without any beating about the bush, I will tell you the story of the secret that I alone hold within my shaggy breast." Here he struck his great broad chest with such a whack that there was quite a hollow rumble and a rasping of his claws, which silenced the whispering of the animals and the twittering of the birds, who were all excited and eager to hear the storyteller.

"I will tell you," he went on in his soft growling voice, "of how I came to be the only one who knows the truth about the crown jewels of the Czar of all the Russias. No one else knows it now, as the few who did are dead. No one but I and the desperate characters who enacted it saw the incident that I am going to unfold to you. I cannot tell you the name of the Czar who was on the throne for I have a bad memory for names, but I do remember that he was a mighty fine, handsome fellow with a high crown to his head and a truly terrible presence that made everyone quail; even his bravest enemies were abashed by the look of fire in his eyes. It was many years ago when he came to the throne as a young man, strong and full of ideals, a dreamer with a look of scorn that betokened that he was not to be trifled with. Indeed he was not, for I have seen him pick up a serf and throw him from a balcony in the banqueting chamber into the street below for so small a fault as the spilling of a drop of wine on the embroidered sleeve of his master's golden coat.

"You may wonder what I was doing near such an exalted figure. Well, I was there to make him laugh, and laugh I made him. I did my job so well and was so jocular that I lived in a corner of the great banqueting hall, at his elbow at every meal, chained by a silver collar set with lumps of jade and amber to a ring in the wall. Here I slept too, comfortable enough on a palliasse of sweet straw, close to a great fire of logs that burned day and night, winter and summer, the whole year through. I had rich juicy bones thrown me from my master the Czar's table and always a bowl of warmed milk and honeycomb stood by my side. I grew plump and sleek and had to dance to please the Czar a great deal or I should have become fat and ill-conditioned.

"I had come into the Czar's possession originally by being part of a coronation present given to him by a rich merchant from Kamchatka. He had given him a veritable zoo. I come of a race of bears who are so tame that the peasant women are not afraid to gather sticks at the very mouths of our lairs, for we do not come near them or molest them, only approaching them to receive food from their hands. However, the excessive tameness of my race procures us no exemption from the persecutions of mankind; many and varied are the ways they inflict pain on us to complete our capture or destruction. With faggots they close up our dens and choke us to death with smoke; with sharpened stakes hidden in the ground they contrive to impale us; with boards hammered all over with evil hooks that they place in our unsuspecting paths they entangle us; and with swinging logs of such weight that, when pushed aside to uncover some spot where men know we find honey, they return with such force as to crush our skulls in.

"Many of my relations have I seen killed in one of these ways and all because we are of so much use to the miserable Kamchadales who so persecute us. For they make bed clothes and hats from our pelts, and shoe soles for their ice boots; they extract great nourishment from our fat, eat out flesh, make sickles to cut grass from our shoulder blades, and masks from the scraped lining of our intestines to protect the faces of their womenkind from the strong rays of the sun. Our heads they hang up as ghastly trophies around their houses and are even beholden to us for what herbs to use to heal their hurts, for they watch our behavior most closely when we are wounded and note which plants we use to cure ourselves. Besides which they copy all our actions and postures in a ridiculous dance they perform called the bear dance. Such is their gratitude, I say, that they serve us with unkindness and death; such is the behavior of mankind toward the brute beast and even toward each other, for they behave with equal treachery as I will show you in my story, which I must continue without more ado." Here the other animals nodded their heads and made noises of agreement.

"When presented to the Czar I was paraded with all the other presents around the great cathedral where he was to be crowned. It was a wonderful sight to see so many richly dressed men and women, representing all the countries of the world, standing hushed in silence while a huge choir sang the most beautiful songs in praise of the new monarch. Great banners hung from the vaulted roof half hidden by blue clouds of sweet-smelling incense; golden and silver faces peered from the gloomy mosaics and holy icons that lined the walls. Richly jeweled candlesticks held the fattest candles to give light to this scene of glittering splendor. The most impressive thing I saw that memorable day was when the Czar's two favorites poured a great bowl of gold coins, in a continuous stream, over his head and shoulders until he was surrounded by a pile of riches reaching to his very knees. There he stood, holding his orb and scepter, staring straight ahead, unflinching, seeming to look into the farthest corners of Russia and to the bottom of the deepest hearts of the most crafty of his congregation. It was a sight to behold, rivaling the feast that followed in its brilliance and magnificence.

"At the banquet the guests sat at an enormous table in the form of the letter T. At the head sat the Czar and his affianced bride; on each side of him stood his favorite friends as cup bearers. Along the length of the huge hall stood the massive oak table, set with golden dishes and jeweled goblets, where sat the relations of the Czar and his bride, the high dignitaries of the church, and the foreign ambassadors who were asked especially so that they could take home tales of all the splendor to make their countrymen envious. In the center of the table stood a great pile of exotic fruit, brought from goodness knows where, the like of which had never been seen in icy Russia before: pineapples and bananas, grapes and melons, pomegranates and figs, and the largest peaches you can imagine. The floor was strewn with herbs and rushes, among them lean borzois and massive deerhounds lay beneath the table, waiting at their master's feet for any chance tidbit, their growls adding to the din as they quarreled among themselves over the bones. The whole scene was lit by smoking torches fixed in hoops of iron on the stone walls. The beams of the roof were hidden in a thick pall of smoke and the smell of resin and burning wood was thick on the air.

"Processions of serfs carried in dishes of food concocted to whet the appetite of even the most surfeited gourmet. Tureens of borscht and salt cucumber soup; roasted peacocks with their gorgeous tails still spread out behind them; whole swans, their milk-white necks arched and garlanded; a boar's head holding in its mouth a lemon and bedecked with sprigs of bay and rosemary; bream sprinkled all over with herbs and horseradish; sturgeon with wine and cherries; pickled fish both large and small decorated with slices of gherkin and lemon; whole suckling pigs roasted to a succulent brownness; great dishes of blini, sour cream, and caviar; barrels of oysters; geese stuffed with nuts, ducks stuffed with salt mushrooms; and a raised pie that must have held several hundred hares, for it took four men to carry it. In and out and around the hall the processions wove—flagons of vodka and kvass were emptied and filled time out of number. Dishes were filled and greedily emptied, grease spilled and gravy splashed; for I may say that the table manners of these bishops and nobles would have been more at home in the stables.

"The meat and fish being consumed, a procession of beautiful girls entered carrying iced cakes and bowls of honeycomb, dishes of white curd and cream, jugs of sweet syrup, canisters of sugar, slabs of a sickly-sweet substance made of dried fruit and nuts powdered all over with sugar and sweet spices, almond paste, piles of rich fruit crystallized in sugar, jars of Chinese ginger, boxes of figs from Smyrna, and a hundred other delicacies I had never seen before and knew not the names of. All the time the Czar and his visitors drank heavily and called for more; all the time the soft sounds of dumkas and balalaikas filled the air; now and again a troupe of dancers, clad in soft muslins all a-jangle with little coins, dashed in to execute the complicated measures of a Russian dance to the cheers and huzzahs of the company.

"When the banquet was over and the remains of the feast cleared away, a procession of serfs carried in the costly jewels that had been used at the Czar's coronation to be admired by the assembled company before they were stowed away once more in the depths of the treasure room that led out of the great banqueting hall itself. All the treasure caves of the East seemed to have come alive in this long solemn procession. The orb made from a gigantic carbuncle studded with huge pearls and surmounted by a cross of uncut diamonds. The scepter made from an ivory tusk entirely covered with alternate rings of rubies and amethysts, topped with a star of topaz. Tiaras of opals and pearls set among rows of diamonds and arcs of crystal. Crowns of pure emeralds, necklaces of sapphires as big as pigeons' eggs, ropes and tassels of pearls. All these passed through a low arch into the treasure chamber, guarded on each side by a tall, black-booted, bewhiskered cossack. The last two serfs carried, one a great bowl of honey and the other a chest of precious stones. Each guest was invited to dip his or her fingers into the honey and then into the coffer of precious stones; all that stuck to them were their own to take away with them as souvenirs of this memorable day.

"One by one the guests left and one by one the torches guttered and went out, until only two remained to light the scene of these departed glories. The Czar's favorites conducted his bride to her chamber leaving the Czar scowling down the length of his depleted banqueting board, alone with the guards of his treasure. Taking a sliver of wood from one of the torches, he lit two candles at an ivory icon and knelt in prayer on a mat of deerskin. Wrapped in his ermine cloak, he was silent for a while, then grabbing his smoking torch he strode from the room, followed by his faithful elkhound, slamming the iron-studded door with such a clang that it woke the sleeping serfs and sent them all scampering away to bed.

"Now I was left with the debris of the feast and the immovable giants who guarded the jewels. Filling myself with scraps of meat and what fruit I could reach, I settled down in my warm corner to sleep contentedly and cogitate on what I had seen that day.

"I know not how long I slept but I awoke at the sound of a creaking door hinge, for I am a very light sleeper especially after a late meal. All was now deathly quiet, the last torch had gone out, the gloom high up in the rafters was gently curdled by the flickering of the dying fire. Dimly I could see that the two bearded giants who were supposed to guard the Czar's jewels were fast asleep, slumped forward on their swords in an attitude of abandon, no doubt brought on by drinking too much kvass. Once more I heard the creak and through half-closed eyes I could see the door that led to the antechamber slowly opening. Keeping my head down and remaining motionless, I watched with thumping heart.

"Around the door came first a hand and then a foot and then a face, which I recognized even in the shadows as the face of one of the Czar's favorites. 'O treacherous man, the favored friend of a mighty Czar, what felony are you plotting, what villainy are you and your friend about?' thought I, for there behind him was the other favorite. Stealthily, wearing their snow overboots and carrying sharp daggers, they crept into the room. Strangest of all things—they were carrying the emerald crown, the ivory scepter, and the pear-topped orb, which I had seen so recently carried into the treasure room by the Czar's servants. Silently they passed the besotted guards, disappearing from view through the door of the treasure chamber. In a moment they reappeared still carrying the royal coronation jewels. One of them glanced guiltily at me, but could not see my open eyes through my overhanging locks. 'But what were they doing, what did this midnight parade of the crown jewels back and forth mean?' I asked myself.

"Stopping in the middle of the hall for one of them to drain a horn of vodka, they held a whispered conversation. The whole of it I could not catch, but from words like 'death,' 'banishment,' 'genuine' or 'counterfeit,' and 'friend,' 'anger,' 'thief,' and from their tone also, I knew them to be quarreling, and about something of a desperate nature. With furtive looks at the icon and greedy glances at the jewels they held in their hands, they talked excitedly in the firelight, then calming each other they walked stealthily from the hall, carefully shutting the door behind them.

"It was then, when it was too late, that I realized that I had witnessed a daring robbery. Gradually it was all clear, the words I had heard like separate links all fitted together into a complete chain. 'Death' if they were discovered. 'Banishment' for their families. 'Genuine' the jewels they had carried out, and 'counterfeit' those they had carried into the treasury. 'Friends' they were of the Czar, his 'anger' if their treachery was discovered; finally 'thieves' that they themselves were. Hence their guilty looks at the icon and the secret way they behaved.

"I ought to have given the alarm, but it was too late. What was the good of roaring out now and waking the guards? They would only belabor me with the flat of their swords for disturbing their rest and I could not tell them what had happened for they would not have understood my language as you do. By now, thought I, the thieves must be safe at home dividing their spoils and breaking up the settings of the jewels so that they could not be recognized when they tried to sell them. What perfidy! The two best friends of the Czar had conspired together to rob the man to whom they should have been most grateful, at whose hands they received such favors. But such is the duplicity of man, to rob his best friend in the dead of night, then to embrace him with smiles of friendship the next day. What a hive of intrigue and mistrust the Czar was living in! He would do well to show his power early and strengthen his guards with tried men he could trust, not drunken louts who slept at their post allowing him to be robbed. No one will suspect, I reflected, that the substitution has taken place, and so no one will probably ever know. As the crown jewels are so seldom used, and not likely to be examined very closely for years, the theft may lie hidden for the rest of time.

"As the first cold light of dawn shone through the narrow windows of the hall, the guards awoke, and yawning assumed positions of attention as if they had been immovable for hours. Not long afterwards they were relieved and withdrew from the banqueting hall. Noises of serfs and nobles getting up soon reached my ears, and the doors were flung open to admit the two villainous friends, who arrived with a golden ewer of water. They had come to wake their friend and master, to perform his ablutions. They showed no outward sign of their perfidy, save for a slightly haggard look about their eyes that only I knew was not caused by the carousals of the night before, but was the stamp of deceit. They bore a shifty insecure look that only I could read. While I watched, they talked with the Czar all day as the best of friends, ate from the same dish, poured his wine, and broke his bread, showing themselves to me in all ways as the most false and treacherous of men. I nursed my secret and growled fiercely at them if they approached me.

"Years went by and no one discovered the theft. The Czar

wore his crown and carried his scepter on several occasions, but never suspected that they were counterfeit. He never knew that the money received from the merchants of Moscow for each jewel from his regalia had gone to swell the ill-gotten gains of his two best friends. In the course of time, the two guards who had been on duty at the treasury door on that fateful night were killed in a battle against the Kurds. One of the Czar's friends was poisoned by the other in a fit of anger. The remaining one was stabbed by the Czar himself for paying unwanted attentions to his Czarina. With their deaths, I was left the only living being who knew that the royal regalia that was used to crown the Czars of Russia was fake and counterfeit, worthless pieces of colored glass set on false mountings.

"I know not if the theft was afterwards discovered or if the things remain as they were until this day, for at the Czar's death I was sold, as no one else liked me; I knew too much about each man's secret life, for I had been the dumb witness of more than one deception.

"After many adventures both pleasant and unpleasant, I came to this shop, in which we shall all remain as in a monastery shut off from the rest of the world, at peace until we catch the fancy of some passerby and once more change hands to be launched out on the turbulent waters of adventure."

On this thoughtful note he ended his tale of deception and theft, leaving his audience, who had expected a gayer tale, somewhat saddened. With a snap of disapproval the dodo announced that on the Sabbath he would tell them a more suitable story, leaving them all wondering what it would be about.

The Quizzits, each with different feelings, trooped off to bed. The children sank almost immediately into a dreamless sleep. Arabella lay dreaming fitfully, crying out as she thought of the work entailed for the servants as they prepared the Russian Czar's banquet. Joseph lay cogitating deeply—he must get to the bottom of this nightly storytelling, and he resolved that they would all listen to the dodo and then he would make their presence known and ask a question or two of the venerable chairman, whom he both respected and loved.

## Chapter VIII

# NIGHT THE SEVENTH . . . SUNDAY
# . . . THE DODO'S TALE

*N*EXT day being Sunday, the shop was as usual closed. No maid came on that day and everything remained silent until noon when the Quizzits, having overslept, crept shamefacedly downstairs. Arabella cooked breakfast, which they ate instead of their accustomed midday repast of roast meat and pudding. Silas, who if allowed to would have slept all day, was surprised and puzzled at the late hour of his awakening by a shout from Mr. Quizzit. But not being very inquisitive he soon forgot it as he went about his Sunday afternoon work of cleaning out all the cages and giving the animals fresh straw bedding. This he had to do alone, as Mr. Quizzit had dozed off in his rocking chair and did not help him. By the evening, when the boy had finished, he too was tired and quite content to go early to rest. The animals had become rather bad-tempered and fidgety as they waited eagerly for the night to fall, when they knew they were going to hear the seventh and last story—the dodo's tale.

Unaware that the whole Quizzit family was listening from behind the stair's door, the dodo began in a soft creaking voice that sounded all dusty and cobwebby through not being properly aired. None of the other animals could ever remember his having spoken more than a few words at a time before the commencement of the storytelling. As chairman he had made regular interjections and now started, with serious intent, to comment on the preceding speakers and their tales.

"We have listened," he began in a ponderous and patronizing tone, "to six very different stories. I cannot say that I approve of all that has been said, nor condone the behavior of some of the characters in the stories. I do not like tales of revenge, villainy, and deception." Here the raccoon, the parrot, and the bear looked, each in their different ways, toward their chairman as if they were going to be called to give an account of themselves.

The raccoon scowled and muttered to himself, for nothing would change his nature no matter what anyone said.

The parrot fluffed out his feathers, cocking his head on one side and winking his inscrutable little eyes as he opened and closed his hooked beak, chuckling all the while quietly to himself.

The bear smiled blandly around at the assembled company taking no notice of the dodo's implied criticisms.

"However," went on the dodo after a prolonged pause, "these frailties were in some measure counterblanced by the promise of happiness expected by the butterflies, and the breaking of the enchantment of the two apricot trees. But on the other hand, we can only feel an abounding pity for our friend Clarissa, who suffers a double imprisonment in the form of an animal and furthermore an animal who is not free."

His listeners looked from one to another questioningly. This was not quite the kind of story they had been expecting and they were all beginning to become impatient.

"You must forgive me," went on the dodo apologetically, almost as if he could read their thoughts, "if you have difficulty in hearing me, for I am not practiced in the ways of public speaking; in fact I am not used to the ways of speech at all. I regard the spoken word as something to be indulged in very rarely and then only if one has something very well worth imparting to one's listener."

Everyone moved closer to their bars; you could almost hear the concentration it was so intense. The dodo cleared his throat a great deal and clicked his tongue as he stood with eyes shut. When at last his voice did come out again it was much less rusty, and as one of the mice whispered to its neighbor he must have swallowed the cobwebs.

"First I must tell you a little of my life and relate how I became somewhat of a philosopher, for when I was younger I was far from being the serious bird that I now am. I was hatched on a coral island of great beauty. From the security of a large nest of dried palm leaves I could gaze on the bluest of blue skies, the most luxuriant green foliage, and watch the most golden sands lapped by a smiling sea. My parents, having attended to my early needs, soon left me to my own devices and it was not long before I quitted the narrow confines of my nest and set out to investigate the world. I soon found, although I am reluctant to admit it, that the other dodos who lived on this island were excessively stupid. I learned from my parents that because of this inherited lack of intelligence the numbers of our race had become very scarce and ours was the last surviving colony of our species. My ancestors had fallen prey over the centuries to the ravages of both men and beasts who had taken advantage of our trusting natures, our laziness, and our vanity.

"Far back, long before I or my parents could remember, dodos had been able to fly like other birds. But gradually, almost without our noticing it, this ability had been lost, until at the time when I emerged from the egg no one had any knowledge of how to fly or what it was like to do so. When I was young I watched with envy the skuas and the albatrosses as they swooped and dived over the sea and land as easily as the breezes blew through the palm leaves. Being of an inquiring turn of mind, I talked a lot to my elders in order to become informed about the history of our race. There was one very venerable dodo, to whom I never tired of listening, who told me tales of long ago and for whom I had a great respect. With tears in his eyes he would tell me stories of how our race had diminished, in particular of one disaster that depleted our numbers very drastically and from which we had never recovered.

"A certain vain and stupid king had caused a huge palace to be built to his own glory constructed entirely of dodos' eggs. To begin with, his masons and carpenters had used only shells from which our ancestors had hatched, but as the palace grew the King became more thoughtless and used unbroken eggs, creating a work of great beauty, intricacy, and originality. But accidents, of which there were many owing to the delicate nature of the building material, caused more and more eggs to be used. When finally the whole edifice was destroyed by a hurricane, the ensuing havoc so enraged the monarch that in his blind fury he blamed the disaster on the dodos and banished them from his kingdom. The ravages he had made on their eggs, and the hardships they suffered as refugees, so depressed the remainder of the dwindling dodo population that they began to sink rapidly into extinction.

"The island of my birth became the last stronghold of dodo life. There my forebears attempted to reestablish a thriving colony; all went well, and slowly they began to increase. It was even thought that some progress had been achieved in learning once more the difficult art of flying. I even remember when I was a chick watching the adolescent dodos painstakingly trudging up the dunes and then rushing headlong down, desperately flapping their wings in what always ended in fruitless effort. By losing the full use of our wings we had lost half of our freedom and this, as I was soon to learn, was of paramount importance."

Some of the birds opened and shut their wings in silent embarrassment. The dodo looked around at this discreet sound and, as if in answer, bowed his beak and shook his wings ineffectually. Then, looking up, he went on.

"I realize now that one of the most terrible events in the history of our race, as related to me by the old dodo, occurred when our island was discovered by an evil band of pirates. They began to use it as a headquarters from which to plan their crimes and as a place to hide the treasures that they stole from other travelers on the high seas. For all I know, the man who found our home may have been Il Tabaro himself, of whom the parrot has told us, or one of his crew set up on his own account. At all events, they began a wanton destruction of us dodos whenever they visited the island. They captured us and carried us off as curiosities, they chased the old birds until they died of exhaustion, and—I can hardly bring myself to mention it—they even slaughtered us and made us into pies."

Here several of the more delicate animals were seen to be having an attack of the vapors, while one very sensitive dutch rabbit fainted and had to be noisily revived by its companions.

After this interruption the dodo spoke more precipitantly.

"I will not continue too long with the details of how I became the last surviving dodo, for they are in truth of great pain to me."

The animals looked from one to another; some heaved sighs of relief, for they were finding the sad and pompous voice of the dodo, droning on in his dry, ponderous style, somewhat boring. Some of them were even yawning and whispering among themselves.

"There came a day," continued the dodo, surreptitiously wiping away a tear from his beak, "when despite my calling up and down the beach I received no reply. I realized at long last that I was alone. Here I was on an island paradise surrounded by the abundance of nature, warmed by the sun yet imprisoned by my own loneliness. I became timid and ill at ease hiding myself among the palms at the slightest unusual noise, and when one day I perceived a ship flying the skull and crossbones with a boatload of men leaving it for my beach, I hid myself in the deepest cave. Every now and again I peered from behind the rocks to see what was going on. I was too far away and too frightened of exposing myself and being observed to be able to see exactly what the pirates were doing, but I presumed as they were digging in the sand that they were once more burying some treasure. After many hours I watched the longboat returning to their ship, and eventually came out of hiding as the pirate craft disappeared over the horizon. I ran posthaste down to the shore to investigate the activities of my unwelcome visitors. As I got nearer I beheld a strange sight—there sticking out of the hot sand was the head of a young man.

"He was unconscious and already dreadfully affected by exposure to the sun. He was obviously a fine specimen of the human race, for what I could see of him emerging from the sand was far more noble than the faces of the pirates, who were the only human beings I had ever seen. Whereas they were dark and pockmarked, with faces distorted by evil thoughts of crime, he was fair and comely with an expression of gentleness and peace. His lowered lids swept healthy cheeks with long lashes, and I felt that he must be a good man or the wicked pirates would not

have abandoned him thus. I bent down and listened to see if he
still lived. Faint, very shallow breaths issued from his parched
lips and I knew that I must hurry. I ran as fast as my claws
would carry me to a spring of fresh water among the palms,
puzzling, as I went, how to revive him. When I got there I
surprised some monkeys who were drinking; frightened by my
sudden appearance, one timorous monkey threw the broken
coconut he was carrying at me before he saw that I meant no
harm. It did not hit me but as it fell into the shallow water it
gave me the idea I needed. Grasping it firmly in my beak I filled
it with water and, more slowly this time, returned balancing the
precious liquid as carefully as I could.

"The young man was in an extreme state of exhaustion and I
had to make several journeys, splashing his head with the water
each time, before I could revive him sufficiently to enable him to
open his eyes. As soon as he had done this I began to make a
little shelter of palm leaves between him and the sun. Never
before had I wished so profoundly that I had hands or even
proper wings, my progress was so terribly slow. When the
young man opened his eyes and saw me peering down at him he
seemed at first too astonished to speak, and I took it that it was
because I had the face of a dodo and not that of a pirate with a
black patch and tobacco-stained teeth."

" 'Good bird,' said the young man faintly, 'I thank thee with
all my heart. Do you but take my hat that lies yonder and fill it
with water, for it will hold more than your coconut shell and I
could do with a good long drink.'

"Gladly I ran for more water as he suggested and then, urged on by his encouraging words, I set about scraping with my claws at the sand that entrapped him. As he continued to revive and was able to communicate with me I learned that the ship on which he had been traveling had been raided and because of his youth and strength the pirate crew had taken him aboard and forced him to join their company. But once there, he had done all he could to hinder their evil trade. Being a forceful young man, he had made a great nuisance of himself until the captain had given orders for him to be made to walk the plank. The rest of his men, however, thought it unlucky to end a man's life thus who had once sailed with them, and they prevailed on the captain to abandon him in this brutal fashion on my island, which for some strange reason they considered was not such an ill-starred end.

"As I worked to release him his gratitude knew no bounds. He vowed, as I brought him fruit and more water to refresh himself, that he would do anything within his power to repay me. Toward sunset he at last wriggled free, and exhausted we both sank senseless onto the sand. When I awoke the night had come and gone, my sailor friend was nowhere to be seen; at first, but for the hole in the sand I thought I had been dreaming but when I went in search of my breakfast I came upon him swimming cheerfully in the lagoon, and a fine-looking young fellow he proved to be.

He thanked me again prodigiously for saving his life and together we went on a tour of the island. He was soon of the opinion that despite the charms of my domain it was without doubt essential that we should escape from it. Knowing nothing of the rest of the world, I had accepted my life there, until I learned from him the freedom I could enjoy should we be successful in our bid to escape. Talking to him, a man of similar intelligence to myself, had opened up new prospects hitherto unknown to me. I heard of the wondrous things in the world and realized that never again could I accept the cage that my island home had become. I must go with him and learn what freedom had to offer, what hopes, what fears, what responsibilities. I knew not then, as I now do, that even when one is free life has its problems.

"However, without more ado I assisted him to construct a strange but strong craft on which we pinned our hopes of release. It was in the form of a raft made on two huge logs shaped by the crude tools that my ingenious new friend had contrived. The day came when, piled high with breadfruit and fresh water, our raft was ready for launching. I stationed myself on it like a figurehead, while its constructor waded into the sea pushing it before him until once in deep water he scrambled aboard. Our journey to freedom had begun. I could not bring myself to look behind me at the land that had given me birth but stared ahead expectantly, my beak and eyes stung by the salt sea spray."

The dodo fell silent. Some of the smaller birds slept on their perches. The mice were becoming restive. The Quizzit family stirred in the hiding place on the stairs. Clearing his throat he once more resumed briskly, for he had noticed that his audience was no longer attentive.

"I will tell you on another occasion of the adventures that befell us before we were picked up by a French cutter bound for France, and of the trials and tribulations that overtook us on our journey to England. Arrive however in London we eventually did, and to the shop belonging to the parents of my young friend we speedily repaired. It was, I can now divulge to you, Mr. Quizzit's great-great-grandfather who had rescued me and brought me home with him to share whatever the future brought forth."

Here the dodo coughed and paused, cocking his eye toward the stair's door behind which he had detected a slight shuffle. The animals, birds, and reptiles all leaned forward, eager to hear what was coming next, when suddenly they were startled by a clang and a flash of unexpected sunshine. Without anyone noticing it, the dawn had broken and Silas was already taking down the shutters.

"What next, what next?" they cried urgently, but too late. Already the muttering dodo had, in company with the ape and the bear, swiveled around to face the window. All they could hear were the unintelligible clickings of the dodo's tongue against his horny old beak.

But this was not the end, for the Quizzit family, to the astonishment of all the animals, pushed open the door and walked into the shop. The parrot had always half expected to see Theodosia and Verney but even he was surprised to see their parents also.

The dodo, the ape, and the bear all turned back to face the shop and as Mr. Quizzit stood smiling, the eyes of all the other animals were on the dodo, to whom everyone looked for an explanation.

"What, may I ask," said Mr. Quizzit in the kindest of tones, "is the meaning of all this?"

# Chapter IX

# HOW IT ALL ENDED

NOW the storytelling was all over. The raccoon had made them laugh. The parrot had made them wonder. The ape had made them cry. The caterpillars had enchanted them. The golden carp had intrigued them. The bear had enthralled them, while the dodo had disquieted and upset them with his talk of freedom, even if his story had been disappointing. Some of them had been in the shop so long that they had forgotten what it was like to run in the early morning through the summer dew, or to cower in some hole or nest as the winter weather gripped the countryside in its relentless grasp. Some of them had never known freedom, for they had been born in their present circumstances and thoughts of what the outside world was like confused and even frightened them. But none the less they longed for the opportunity to taste what it had to offer.

"What is the meaning of all this?" repeated Mr. Quizzit, confronting his old friend the dodo. For a moment the ancient bird looked as if he was not going to speak, but then cocking his head on one side and fixing Mr. Quizzit with one of his great big eyes he said:

"We came to this arrangement in order to keep down the racket, so that you and your family could rest and be in the best of tempers and therefore treat us as well as we could expect to be treated by human beings in our confinement."

"Have we not always treated you well?" replied Mr. Quizzit in a wounded manner, looking from the animals to his family who stood around him. "I have never sought to confine you. You have always chosen to live in the shop with your animal companions," he went on, addressing his remarks to the dodo.

"Ah, yes, you have always been very kind. The man Quilt, as we have heard in the raccoon's tale, was the only one to be brutal, and everyone will admit that as soon as you became aware of his cruelty you turned him out of doors."

"Well, then, what is it you want?" queried Mr. Quizzit.

"Free us," cried the dodo in the loudest tones he had ever been heard to use.

"Freedom," echoed a hundred voices behind him, "happiness, peace, freedom . . . give us our liberty."

The ape looked particularly doleful and presented such a spectacle of misery that Theodosia ran over and put her arms about her for comfort. The bear also hung his head until Verney ran toward him and nestled in his arms. Mrs. Quizzit took her husband's hand and squeezed it, drawing his attention to the touching picture of the two children and the two animals comforting one another.

"Can nothing be done?" said Arabella to her husband. "It seems dreadful that the poor dodo came all this way from his island to find freedom and now is shut up in this dark shop. Is there nothing we could do to help all the others who wait for customers to take them away?" The silence in the shop at these words was as it had never been before.

Mr. Quizzit patted his wife's hand but gently shook his head.

"How could we live?" he said. "I have no other trade and I am too old a dog to learn new tricks. The animal business has always been mine and my father's before. I know no other. I live for animals, in a manner of speaking."

"Well, live for us and let us go," said the raccoon bad-temperedly.

"Free us," cried the butterflies and the small birds. Consternation followed the previous silence.

"But how could we live?" repeated Mrs. Quizzit imploringly. Amidst the hubbub of suggestions that ensued Mr. Quizzit realized that the ape-princess was trying to communicate something to Theodosia that the child could not understand. The poor dumb creature was looking beseechingly at Mr. Quizzit and tugging at something on her hairy finger as she made plaintive moaning sounds. Mr. Quizzit went to her, and taking her horny hand in his, asked kindly what ailed her. For answer two huge tears like pearls from her princess's crown trickled from her sorrowful eyes and fell on their clasped hands. Mr. Quizzit looked down and moved his other hand to brush them away, when he saw what Clarissa was trying to draw their attention to. Nestling in her long hair shone the green ring that the Princess with the glass feet had given her faithful friend the ape. Slipping it off her finger, Mr. Quizzit held it up for all to see. The ape for the first time since she had been in the shop jumped and smiled with excitement.

"Is it magic?" cried Theodosia. The ape shook her shaggy head, but in such a way as to invoke more questions.

"Is it valuable?" asked Arabella.

"Worth a king's ranson, I'll be bound," growled the bear who, as his story had borne out, had some experience in these matters.

The dodo looked very reflective, and then with a dusty rattle of his feathers and a dry clicking of his beak he spoke:

"It is indeed worth a king's ransom. It is the answer to our problem. Sell it and we can all live in luxury for the rest of our lives." Having thus spoken this sentence, he seemed to shrink and become older in a moment. They were the last words he was ever heard to utter.

"Brilliant," cried Mr. Quizzit. "I'll do it. We'll sell the ring, sell the shop, and buy a farm deep down in the country where we can all be happy. Those animals who want to stay with us may do so and those who want to go free can go."

"Hurrah!" cried all the animals, birds, fishes, insects, and even the chrysalides who wriggled and twitched. Never was such a noise heard before in St. Paul's Churchyard.

Joseph Quizzit was a man of his word, and in the morning he took the ring to Hatton Garden where a rich jewel merchant nearly died of apoplexy when he saw the stone. Silas and Mr.

Quizzit had to borrow another wheelbarrow to take the sacks of gold sovereigns straight to Coutts' Bank, so heavy were they and so numerous.

Then began the business of clearing up. It was soon decided that the bear, the ape, and the dodo would spend the rest of their days with the Quizzits at Cherry Tree Farm, which Mr. Quizzit had found in the heart of Suffolk. It was situated down a long lane on the side of a hill, bathed in sunshine, sheltered from the winds, and a paradise of cherry blossoms in the springtime.

The parrot, sad to relate, had fallen a victim to the shock of their good fortune and had been given to the taxidermist, who made him into part of Mrs. Montague's famous feather hangings.

The raccoon could not be persuaded to give up his revenge and he had gone off at first light on the day after the gift of the ring in search of his enemy Quilt.

The caterpillars turned into chrysalids, and the chrysalids into butterflies, and as the cortege of Quizzits traveled along the road from London to Suffolk, bright butterflies could be seen winging their way up into the azure sky as Arabella and Theodosia set them free.

Verney had been allowed to loose all the mice and rats in St. Paul's Churchyard and they had gone snuffling and squeaking off across the gravestones, wrinkling their noses and twitching their whiskers; except one piebald mouse who didn't want to go free and who to his great delight had run straight up Verney's sleeve and lodged itself inside his shirt, from whence it refused to budge.

The fish were tipped carefully into the lake in St. James's Park—where they are to this day, some very old, some the great-great-grandchildren of the ones from Mr. Quizzit's shop.

The week before the family moved, Mr. Quizzit and Silas went down to Cherry Tree Farm and fitted up one of the barns into a dormitory for the remaining animals. They brought with them one of the sacks of sovereigns, which the bear was proudly going to guard so that Mr. Quizzit would not have to go constantly to the Bank in London and so that he would be able to visit Hadleigh market weekly to buy provender for them all.

The family moved to Suffolk with all their belongings piled onto four carts that Mr. Quizzit hired from a flour miller of his acquaintance. On the first cart rode the family with Mr. Quizzit driving; on the second, the three chosen animals with old Mr. Quizzit, Joseph's father, at the reins, who had not wanted to be left behind in Mortlake so far from his son and grandchildren; on the third, the furniture and the little maid-of-all-work, with Silas driving; and on the fourth, the flour miller, like Noah surrounded by the animals and birds who were to be released in the country or who because of their remote homes were going to stay with the Quizzits until they decided what they wanted to do. In this cart also rode three of the miller's men who were to drive the wagons back again to London.

As they drove along, Theodosia and Verney fell to discussing the stories the animals had told.

"We never heard the first two tales," said Verney regretfully.

"No," said Theodosia, "but the parrot said it was all about the raccoon's spiteful revenge on the man Quilt who used to work for father before Silas came."

"I wonder if that was fun," replied Verney in a not-very-interested voice.

"I shouldn't think so," said Theodosia. "What a lot about how evil human beings are, and how deceitful, there was in the bear's tale."

"The parrot said that his tale was all about knavery too," said Verney. "Anyone would think to hear those animals talk that we did nothing but steal from one another all the time."

"Yes, I am afraid they haven't a very good opinion of us," replied his sister. "I loved the ape's tale," she went on, "even if it was sad, and I am sure somehow Clarissa will be happy at Cherry Tree Farm. I feel as if something nice is waiting around the corner for her."

"I do hope so," said Verney. "After all it is her ring that has made it possible for Father to retire," he added seriously.

Theodosia hummed quietly to herself and stroked the cat that sat in her lap.

"Oh well," said Verney, "anyhow the carp's tale had a happy ending and so did the raccoon's, didn't it, even if he was rather spiteful?"

"Yes," agreed Theodosia, "only the raccoon still hasn't finished with Quilt yet." Then after a pause she added, "I must confess that I was getting rather tired of what the dodo had to say."

"So was I," whispered Verney very quietly so that the dodo should not hear and his feelings be hurt.

"But still," said Theodosia leaning forward expectantly, "it was he who first asked Father to free them all." And as she said it, they came in sight of Cherry Tree Farm and all the animals began to get very excited.

As they approached their new home the birds flew on ahead in a brilliant noisy cloud. The monkeys chattered and jumped, nearly overbalancing their traveling boxes. Even the armadillo unrolled and peered out to see their arrival.

No animal ever again lived in a cage. All of them were free. The bear struck up a friendship with a kind traveling peddler and in the summer months he would wander the countryside with him. He carried a pole and danced at the hiring fairs, where he became a great favorite. He was very happy. He slept with his friend in barns, in fields and forests, and when the cold nights came on he returned once more to the welcoming warmth of the Quizzits' home.

The ape Clarissa was visited by a young and handsome nobleman from Tendring Hall, who fetched her once a week in a carriage and took her with him to dine wrapped in a white Kashmir shawl. Whether or not it was her brother nobody ever knew. He was sweet and kind to her and no longer did she grieve in a corner, but she slept in a little brass bed with linen sheets and ran about the fields with Theodosia and Verney twining garlands of cuckoopint and eglantine. She even walked with them to school in Polstead, and the country people soon became accustomed to the sight of her loping home across the fields in all weathers when she had delivered the children to school.

The dodo became very infirm. He seldom went out, ate little, and never spoke. On warm days the Quizzit children helped him into a bathchair and trundled him up and down the stable yard in the sunshine, but it seemed to tire him and so they soon gave up even this. After which he spent all his time in the chimney corner gazing into the embers, his feet in the warm ashes, and his gray feathers mingling with the smoke from the fire. Old Mr. Quizzit bore him company on the other side of the hearth and was almost as silent as the old bird.

Together these two sat in the evening of their days, loved and respected by all around them. While forever after the animals were thankful to Joseph Quizzit and the dodo for giving them, with the help of Clarissa's ring—their FREEDOM.